"Do Y   dall, Take T   Lawful Wedded Husband?"

Jess set her jaw. "I do." Her eyes were locked with Gabe's as she spoke, and she was startled by the open hunger that flared in them, though she shouldn't have been. Gabriel Dumont was a man who held on to what he owned. Of course he'd be possessive with his bride, no matter that she'd been chosen for reasons other than passion.

As far as Gabe was concerned, she'd just become *his*.

She felt herself jerk at a loud cheer and realized she'd missed the rest of the ceremony. As she'd missed the uneasy truth now staring at her—she might've walked into this marriage thinking it a simple bargain, but it was something far more complex.

And far more perilous.

Dear Reader,

When I began this story, I knew that the setting for it had to be a region of unparalleled natural beauty, one so stunning that it would dig its way into a person's heart and make them do almost anything to keep it. I found such a place in the vast open spaces of the Mackenzie Country, which is sometimes called New Zealand's outback.

The Mackenzie is a jewel hidden in the shadow of the Southern Alps and gets its name from an infamous sheep rustler named James Mackenzie, who traveled this mountain area in the nineteenth century. It is a landscape of isolated sheep stations and endless skies, a place where a man might find his courage…and a woman, her true heart.

I hope you enjoy this journey into the wild splendor of the Mackenzie Country.

Take care,

Nalini Singh

NALINI SINGH

BOUND BY MARRIAGE

Published by Silhouette Books
America's Publisher of Contemporary Romance

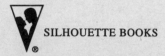 SILHOUETTE BOOKS

ISBN-13: 978-0-373-76781-6
ISBN-10:   0-373-76781-1

BOUND BY MARRIAGE

Visit Silhouette Books at www.eHarlequin.com

Printed in U.S.A.

Books by Nalini Singh

Silhouette Desire

Desert Warrior #1529
Awaken to Pleasure #1602
Awaken the Senses #1651
Craving Beauty #1667
Secrets in the Marriage Bed #1716
Bound by Marriage #1781

NALINI SINGH

has always wanted to be a writer. Along the way to her dream, she obtained degrees in both the arts and law (because being a starving writer didn't appeal). After a short stint as a lawyer, she sold her first book, and from that point there was no going back. Now an escapee from the corporate world, she is looking forward to a lifetime of writing, interspersed with as much travel as possible. Currently residing in Japan, Nalini loves to hear from readers. You can contact her via e-mail, nalini@nalinisingh.com, or by writing to her c/o Silhouette Books, 233 Broadway, Suite 1001, New York, NY 10279.

To Wanda, who makes me a better writer.
And to the Brainstorming Desirables and NZRomance
e-mail groups, who between them, can answer any
research question ever invented!

One

The last person Jess Randall expected to see as she walked out of the arrival gate at Christchurch International Airport, was the man she was about to marry. "Gabriel. What are you doing here?"

"You've been living in L.A. for a year and that's all you have to say?"

Flustered, she leaned forward to drop a quick kiss on his cheek. It felt unfamiliar, awkward. "Sorry, I was just surprised. Aren't you busy with station work?"

"I wanted to talk to you about something. But first things first." He bent his head and, without any prelude, kissed her full on the mouth.

Knocked completely off her bearings, she couldn't do anything but clutch at his shirt in an effort to keep herself upright. Her heart was a staccato drumbeat in her ears, her blood a rush of thunder. And all around

her burned a rough male heat that demanded everything she had.

It was the most intimate kiss they'd ever shared, the
closest their bodies had ever come. And it made her
nerves tighten in sheer panic. Not because she didn't
like it, but because she *did*.

"Welcome home," he said, releasing her. The look in
those green eyes was unmistakable—Gabriel Dumont
was a man more than ready for his wedding night.

Legs not quite steady, she watched him pick up her
bags. He led her through to the domestic part of the
airport and across the road to the landing field used by
smaller planes. The *Jubilee*, one of Angel Station's two
planes, sat waiting for them.

Fear—of Gabe's expectations, but mostly of her own
inexplicable response to his touch—had such a stran-
glehold on her that she was barely aware of hopping on
board. Over the past year, she'd convinced herself that
her marriage would be a calm, steady, business-like
affair, never once considering what it might mean to be
Gabriel's wife in truth…to be touched and claimed in
ways that obliterated the distance she needed to survive
this bargain.

Her heart stuttered as he settled in beside her, taking
the pilot's seat. Taking control. A man who knew what
he wanted and exactly how he wanted it, her fiancé was
not someone who could ever be ignored.

Though he was tall and undeniably strong, his mus-
culature was lean and powerful, not bulky. When he
moved it was like watching a wild stallion in its prime;
healthy and magnificent and proud. The faded burn
scars on his left arm and back took nothing away from
that—they possibly even contributed to the overwhelm-

ing sense of masculinity that surrounded him. Add in the pure green eyes and that sun-shot hair, and it almost seemed as if he'd become more beautiful in the year's absence…more *wrong* for her.

Gabe might have the looks that stopped women in their tracks, but it was the same kind of beauty as that of a tiger in the wild—dangerous and definitely untouchable. Not for the first time, she wondered at the lunacy of her decision to marry a man she knew so little about, notwithstanding that she'd grown up as his neighbor.

"So, what did you learn in L.A.?" he asked, long after they were safely in the air.

Still unsettled by the effect of his kiss, she had to fight to keep her voice calm. "That I can paint."

"We both knew that, Jess. It was why you went to the States in the first place."

"True." She'd wanted to study under renowned painter Genevieve Legraux. "What I meant was I found out I could paint on a level that might support a career." It had been a startling discovery for a woman who'd spent her whole life helping her parents on their small sheep station, snatching only pieces of time for her art.

"Genevieve encouraged me to submit my work to some galleries." She'd even dared send something to Richard Dusevic, an Auckland-based and very well connected gallery owner who could make or break an artist's career.

"You didn't mention that during my calls."

She shrugged, her mind flicking back to those twice-weekly conversations. They'd lasted no more than a few minutes at most but had inevitably left her feeling lost and confused. "I wanted to show you the actual paintings." Because she knew that Gabe took nothing on faith. "They should be arriving soon—I shipped them."

The sun glinted off his hair as he nodded. "Will you miss Los Angeles?"

"No." She looked out the window. They were passing over the patchwork quilt of the Canterbury Plains. Soon they'd be in the Mackenzie Country, a stunning piece of paradise hidden in the shadow of New Zealand's Southern Alps and the only place she'd ever truly called home. "I needed to get out of here for a while but not for always. I'm back to stay."

"Are you?"

Picking up the edge in his tone, she turned from the window. "What kind of a question is that? We're getting married…unless you've changed your mind?" Maybe he'd actually fallen in love with one of those sensual, confident women who graced his bed in an ever-changing parade. Her hands curled into fists at the thought.

"I'm ready." He made a small adjustment to the controls. "It's you I'm worried about."

"I promised I'd return ready for marriage. And I have." Shell-shocked by the twin blows of her father's death and the foreclosure of Randall Station, she hadn't had the strength to be anyone's wife twelve months ago, much less that of a man like Gabriel.

"Damon and Kayla have separated."

Her mind couldn't make sense of the words. "What? But I thought you said Kayla was pregnant."

"Heavily. Your boyfriend walked out on her three months ago."

It was a slap. "Damon is my friend, nothing more." Her fists tightened hard enough to hurt.

"No matter how much you wish otherwise?" He glanced at her, eyes so icy she could see nothing except her own reflection.

"Yes. No matter how much I wish otherwise," she admitted, in spite of her humiliation. "He never loved me, not like he loves Kayla."

"Doesn't much seem like it. The boy's running around with anything in possession of a pair of breasts."

The blunt words brought heat to her cheeks. "He's hardly a boy. He's the same age as me." And twenty-six was plenty old enough to grow up and grow up hard.

"He's acting like a child right now." Gabe ignored her statement. At thirty-five, he was nine years older and the gap was never more apparent than at times such as this.

"How did it happen?" she asked, white noise crashing through her mind. "And why didn't you tell me before?"

He gave her an odd look. "Didn't Damon?"

"What?" She tucked her hair behind her ears. "No, we haven't talked since I left."

"Never?"

"No," she lied, trying not to think of that single phone call Damon had made from a bar four months ago. He'd been drunk, but he'd said things no married man should have said…things she shouldn't have listened to. "Is it looking bad?"

"Rumor is they're heading for divorce."

"Poor Kayla."

"Hypocrisy, Jess? I didn't expect that from you."

Her cheeks blazed anew. "No matter what you think, I wouldn't wish that kind of pain on any woman. Unless…did she ask for the separation?"

"Not from the way she's looking."

"I can't believe Damon would walk out on his marriage."

"Maybe he finally realized what he'd given up."

There was no mistaking the challenge in Gabe's voice. "What are you going to do?"

"Do?" She was still reeling from the implications of his first sentence.

"We're getting married tomorrow and I plan on us staying that way. So if you're intending on chasing off after Damon, you sure as hell better tell me now."

Jess took a shuddering breath and let it out again. "How am I supposed to make any kind of decision right this second?"

"The same way you decided to marry me and use my money to go to L.A."

"Don't you throw that in my face! You agreed to me leaving the area for a year."

Tanned skin pulled tight over the ruthless angle of his jaw. "Answer the damn question. Do you want to get married or not?"

In truth, she didn't really have a choice. If she backed out, she'd lose her last fragile grip on the land that had once been Randall Station. "How much to buy back Randall?" Gabe had never particularly wanted it. The only reason he'd stepped in during the foreclosure was because she'd gone to him begging. But that didn't change the fact that he now owned it. Owned *her*.

He snorted. "You didn't have that kind of money then and you don't have it now. Neither does Damon."

Both undeniable facts. She also owed Gabe for the year in L.A.—a year she'd so desperately needed to grow up. And growing up was exactly what she'd done. She might love Damon, but she'd made a promise to her father on his deathbed and she *would* keep it. A Randall would always remain on Randall land. "I'll marry you."

"You'll be signing a pre-nup."

She heard the unsaid statement loud and clear. "I won't be trying to get the land back in a divorce. You bought it free and clear." And in doing so, he'd saved it from the developers who would have destroyed it completely.

Paying the price he'd demanded—marriage—hadn't seemed like such a sacrifice then. Especially since she'd believed that the marriage would ask nothing from her in terms of emotional commitment, allowing her to keep body and soul safe. *Protected.* It had never crossed her mind that Gabe might not permit her that distance.

Until he'd kissed her.

"My lawyer will bring over the papers tomorrow morning."

"Fine." Gabriel's money itself had never been the thing she was after. It was losing the right to step foot on the very land she'd been entrusted to hold that she couldn't bear.

Silence filled the cockpit. Dropping her head against the seat, she tried to think past the painful knot in her throat. *Damon was separated.* A small, selfish part of her, the part that had loved Damon forever, wanted to tell Gabe to call off the wedding. But she'd stopped lying to herself a long time ago. Even if Damon was acting like a single man again, he'd never once seen her as anything other than his best friend.

To counter that logic her mind insisted on remembering Damon's unexpected phone call, the things he'd said. Swallowing, she fought back with the knowledge that he'd been drinking. He hadn't meant it. *Any of it.* She couldn't afford to think otherwise.

"What's with the weight loss?" Gabe's sharp question cut through the air like a knife.

"It just happened." A combination of grief, shock

and the stress of those first few months in a strange city. "I thought you'd be pleased." Because his women had always been long-limbed, slender beauties. Even now she was short and not quite skinny.

"I'm not marrying you for your body."

She bit her lower lip. "No." Despite that devastating kiss, she knew too well that rich, successful and extremely attractive Gabriel Dumont wasn't marrying her for her body. Nor was he marrying her for her wit or her confirmed knowledge of station life. No, Gabriel was marrying her for one simple, practical reason: unlike every other woman who'd ever crossed his path, she had no romantic illusions about him.

She didn't want or expect him to love her, not now, not ever. And that made her imminently suitable to marry a man who had no ability to love, and didn't want to be bothered with a wife who'd disrupt his life with dreams of romance. "I got a dress in L.A. For the wedding," she said, in an effort to fill the emptiness between them.

Gabriel wasn't buying Jess's apparent calm. "Not the least bit hesitant?"

"You gave me a year. I'm ready now."

I need to find out who I am before I become Mrs. Dumont for the rest of my life...I never learned to stand up for myself and I know I'll have that with you. If I don't, you'll destroy me without meaning to.

Her desperate plea the night they'd made the decision to marry slammed into his mind. The sheltered only daughter of late-in-life parents, she'd still been floundering three months after the loss of her single remaining parent—her father. Yet she'd had the courage to say to Gabe's face what many never would—that he was quite capable of destroying a softer, less powerful personality with the unforgiving pragmatism of his own.

The woman beside him sounded nothing like the broken girl of twelve months ago…except for that underlying thread of courage. "Good," he said, not certain he liked that quiet hint of steel. He'd chosen Jess because he'd known she'd ask less than nothing from him. All she cared about was keeping the former Randall Station in her family.

"You," she said, stopped, then restarted. "You didn't find another woman?"

"I want you to be my wife, Jess. I want you to live on Angel Station, take my name and bear my children." He made sure she heard the determination in his voice—he'd made his choice and he'd stick with it.

The fact she felt nothing for him didn't faze him in the least. He'd decided long ago that love would play no part in any marriage of his. "Unlike Damon, I've kept it in my pants since we got engaged."

"Are you going to throw his name into every conversation we have?"

He glanced over at the unexpected rebuke to catch her with her eyes narrowed and her arms folded. It amused him. She might have grown up a little but Jess was still a featherweight in comparison to him. "Who do you want to invite to the wedding?"

She gave a frustrated sigh and thrust a hand through her hair, sending red curls every which way. He found his eyes lingering on the fiery strands. That was one thing about Jess that hadn't changed—that wild, silky mass of hair so incongruous with her quiet, undemanding personality.

"I'd like to keep it small and if we invite some people

from Kowhai," she named the nearest town, "and not others, it'll cause hard feelings. How about we limit it to the station folk?"

"Nobody else?"

"No," Jess said, wondering if she was imagining the renewed edge in his tone. "Do people…?"

"Some have been guessing since they heard you were coming back and going straight to Angel." He reached to flip a switch and she was transfixed by the pure strength under the golden-brown of his skin. "After the wedding is early enough to confirm the rumors."

Jess nodded, unable to stop thinking that soon Gabe's hands would be touching far more intimate things than the controls of a plane. The thought threatened to reawaken her earlier panic but she forced it down. The day she let that panic show was the day she lost any hope of making this marriage work. Gabriel would never respect a weak woman. "That'll make it easier."

"Four p.m. tomorrow all right for you?"

Her throat was so dry she had to cough lightly to clear it. "Okay." There was no reason to wait—they'd made their bargain on a rainy night a year ago.

Now it was time for her to pay up.

Two

"**I**'ve put your things in the guest bedroom for tonight." Gabe braced his hands on the verandah railing on either side of her, the masculine heat of his chest searing her back.

Her stomach twisted though she knew full well he would never force her. Gabe might be ruthless, but if she said no, he'd back off. And all talk of marriage would end. She'd be escorted off the station with no invitation to ever return.

"Only tonight?" she asked, focusing on the distant grandeur of the Alps. Located in the basin beneath those magnificent behemoths, the Mackenzie stunned even in the final grip of winter. But the aching beauty of her homeland couldn't calm her at this moment. "You can't mean us to…so soon?"

"We're going to be married, Jess."

"I know. But we can't—"

"I was upfront with you about wanting children."

It took every ounce of her courage to continue in the face of his intractable will. "I'm just saying we need time to get used to each other that way."

"What way?" The words were spoken against the sensitive skin of her neck, his breath a hot caress.

Desire flashed through her bloodstream, a shock that threatened to turn her world upside down. "You know what I'm trying to say."

"I've been celibate for a year." A flat declaration. "If you want more time, find another man."

"I can't believe you said that." She tried to turn but he refused to allow it. "You're telling me you'll call off the wedding if I don't agree to have sex with you straight away?"

His body was an inescapable trap around hers. "Think about it, Jess. Why are we marrying? You want to keep the Randall land in your family and I'm thirty-five, at a stage in my life where I want children to ensure Angel Station's future.

"Essentially, we're marrying to provide heirs for both of us. If you're not willing to do what it takes to create them, what's the point? Either we start as we mean to go on or we don't start at all."

It was a brutally practical depiction of their bargain, heartbreaking in its truth. And it made her furious. Why couldn't he have even *tried* to soften things this one time, when she most needed it? "I'm a virgin, Gabe. So if I make a few mistakes tomorrow, you'll have to excuse me."

He went completely, utterly motionless behind her. "What did you say?"

She was at once proud for having caught him off-guard, and more than a touch nervous about her admission. "You heard me."

"Are you telling me Damon never tried anything?"

If he'd had been any other man, she'd have thought the question a deliberate attempt to rub salt into still-open wounds. But sly maliciousness wasn't Gabe's style—he attacked head on. "No."

"And you didn't find another lover?" He answered his own query before she could say anything. "Of course not. You were waiting for Damon to fall in love with you."

His cruel guess cut far too close to the mark. "We both know that didn't happen, so I'm rather less experienced than you might be used to." The understatement of the century. Gabe's women had always had sensuality oozing from their pores, a silent, dark knowledge in their eyes.

"Fine. I'll train you myself."

Stunned, she swiveled in his arms. "That had better have been a joke."

He bent his head until his lips were a hairsbreadth from hers. "I thought you knew—I don't have a sense of humor." His kiss was nothing soft, nothing gentle. Pure male arrogance and resolve, he made her open her mouth for him and when she did, he took her.

No mercy. No holds barred.

As at the airport, Jess froze. But this time, the kiss didn't end in a hard flash. It was an inferno and she found herself clinging to him without knowing how she'd gotten there, her body pressed to his, her mind awash in unadulterated need. When he did release her, it was only so she could gasp in a breath. Then he claimed her again.

And her thoughts scattered like a million grains of sand under a thundering surf.

Gabe took his time tasting Jess, enjoying the lush softness of her mouth. There was no doubt in his mind that she was responding to him on a primal level. It was exactly what he'd set out to achieve. Jess might love another man but she was going to be screaming her husband's name in bed.

What he'd never expected was the exquisite pleasure she gave him in return. That didn't make him happy. Passion had a way of sabotaging the best laid plans, of pushing things off-kilter. In choosing Jess, he'd made the deliberate decision to steer clear of desire. But here she was, wildfire in his arms.

Breaking the kiss, he watched her try to regain control, her breasts rubbing against his chest as she took several ragged breaths. Her lips were wet, her eyes closed and her body pliant. It was tempting to initiate another kiss but he had no intention of ceding power in this arena. Or any other.

Her eyes opened.

Rubbing his thumb over her lower lip, he dropped his other hand to rest on the curve of her hip. "We'll have no problems in bed."

The sweetly feminine submissiveness disappeared in a split-second. "Let me go. You've proved your point."

Releasing her, he stepped back and dropped his eyes to the pebbled hardness of her nipples. A flush streaked up her neck but she didn't make any effort to cover them. Stubborn. He'd delight in taming her. "Get some sleep. It'll be a busy day tomorrow. And Jess, remember, I'm not a man who lets go of what's mine."

Mrs. Croft, the cook and housekeeper for the main house on Angel Station, was bustling about in the kitchen by the time Jess came downstairs at around seven the next morning.

"What's with the sleeping in, Jess my girl?" The older woman bussed her on the cheek. A friend of Jess's mother, she'd known Jess a long time.

Jess rubbed at her face, skin tingling from the cold water she'd used to wash it. "Blame it on the time change. Where's Gabe?" She tried and failed in her attempt not to think about the ruthlessness with which he'd demonstrated her susceptibility to him last night. She shouldn't have been surprised. Gabe had a reputation as an iron-willed adversary in business. Why had she supposed he'd be any different as a husband?

"Gone to check on the stock with Jim." Mrs. C. named the foreman. "The man doesn't seem to realize it's his wedding day and he should be nervous."

Jess almost laughed at the idea of Gabe being nervous about anything. Except today, she had no laughter in her. "Is there anything I can do to help you?" Maybe keeping busy would stop the thoughts pinwheeling through her mind.

The older woman waved away the offer. "Just sit and eat some breakfast. Then you'll be free to pretty yourself up for the wedding."

Jess ate the food that was put in front of her, but had anyone asked her what she'd eaten, she wouldn't have been able to tell them. Her mind was too full of other things. The heart of her, the part that had loved Damon forever, kept insisting that she was making a terrible mistake, that she should walk away from this wedding. Maybe Damon…

No.

Kayla was pregnant. Jess wouldn't be able to live

with herself if something happened to either mother or child because of her actions. And the truth was, Damon had had more than two decades to fall in love with Jess. He'd always chosen someone else.

What about that phone call? The madness in her whispered again. Don't you remember what he— Stop! Screaming silently at her self, she pushed aside the empty plate. "I think I'll go for a walk to clear my head."

Mrs. C. nodded. "Gabe's out by the east barn."

Smiling, Jess thanked her, walked outside and headed west. After last night, her husband-to-be was the last person she wanted to see. Because in those few explosive moments on the verandah, he'd destroyed everything she thought she knew about herself. What kind of a woman loved one man and kissed another with such passionate need?

Two of the sheepdogs ran past, then returned to circle her before deciding to lead the way. The interruption was precisely what she'd needed. Taking a deep, deep breath of the crisp morning air, she focused her attention on the untamed splendor of the land around her— tussock-covered hills dotted with sheep, hardy wildflowers more beautiful than any cultured garden and over it all, an endless blue sky.

Mind and body calmed. This was right. This land was where she was meant to be—everything in her knew it. She could never walk away.

No matter what the cost.

The dogs barked and raced off. She followed at a more leisurely pace, her eye taking in the west barn in the distance. It was the single structure to have survived the catastrophic fire twenty-five years ago. Her father had been one of those who'd come to fight the flames that night, but no one had been able to stop the conflagration. Like a beast let loose from some infernal region, it had devoured almost everything...and everyone.

Having reached the old building, she decided to push open the door and look around, but that was before she saw who was inside. "Mrs. C. said you were in the other barn."

Gabe slammed one hay bale on top of another, sending dust sparkling into the invading sunlight. "So eager to see me?" Pulling off his work gloves, he thrust them into the back pocket of his jeans.

She refused to let him see how much he'd rattled her. "What are you doing here?" And why did her eyes keep going to the sweat-slick muscles of his arms, revealed by the short sleeves of his T-shirt?

"We needed to create some space in here and everyone else was busy."

"Oh." She scuffed the floor with her shoe. "Can I ask you something?"

His answer was a grunt as he shrugged into the sheepskin jacket he'd apparently thrown off earlier. Taking that as a yes, she carried on. "After the wedding sometime, maybe tomorrow or the day after...would you mind if we visited my parents?" They were buried next to each other in the Randall family cemetery, only about a sixty-minute drive away. Although Angel was a huge spread, the family quarters had been built relatively close to those of the adjoining station.

"Of course I don't mind." His face was all harsh masculine lines when he glanced at her, but she thought she heard a buried thread of unexpected gentleness.

His understanding probably wouldn't last through her next request but she was going to start this marriage as she meant to go on—she would not let Gabriel

Dumont crush either her mind or her spirit. "I want to visit your family, too."

Silence.

"I don't have any memories of them, but I know Michael was four, Angelica even younger." No response. She pushed on. "They were your family. We should remember them."

"Fine." It was a flat sound but at least he'd agreed. "You ready for the wedding?" He nodded at the door.

She tugged it open, her palm sweaty in spite of the low temperature. "As ready as I'll ever be."

Stepping out, they began to walk toward the main house.

"We're not going to have time for a honeymoon."

"I understand. That's okay." It was no lie. The idea of being with Gabe 24/7 in some romantic resort tied her stomach up into a thousand knots. She was about to say something else when her attention was caught by a dark blue sedan pulling up to the house. It was followed by an almost identical vehicle in deep green. "Did you invite some other people?"

"That's David Reese, my lawyer." He picked up the pace. "The other car will be Phil Snell, your lawyer."

"Mine?" She nearly had to jog to keep up with him.

"If you sign the pre-nup without independent legal advice, you could challenge it down the road."

"Oh."

They didn't speak the rest of the way. Both lawyers were nice enough at first glance and when Phil took her aside for a private chat, Jess found him to be a very sharp operator. But of course he would be—Gabriel wanted this airtight.

"If you and Mr. Dumont divorce, you'll have no

claim on the land," Phil summarized. "But you'll get a substantial monetary settlement dependent on the duration of the marriage. It's an extremely good deal. Your fiancé is a generous man."

This had never been about money. It was about her heritage, about promises, about loyalty. "Where do I sign?"

Afterward, she walked up to her bedroom, something inexplicably heavy and painful inside of her. It seemed wrong that her wedding day should start like this, with a discussion of money and assets. But what else had she expected? Angel Station was Gabe's heartbeat—as his future wife, she fell somewhere far, far lower on his list of priorities.

"Nothing you didn't already know," she whispered to herself, running her hand down the ivory satin of her wedding dress. So why was she suddenly so sure she was about to make the worst mistake of her life?

"I miss you, Jessie. I should've never let you go. Come back to me…"

Trembling, she picked up the phone, barely aware of what she was doing and began to punch in a number from memory. The first six digits were easy but a single tear streaked down her face as her finger hovered over the last one. *No.* Shaking her head, she hung up before she threw away both her father's memory and her own self-respect in an effort to chase an impossible dream.

A few short hours later, her hand squeezed the delicate stems of her bouquet with crushing force. Having Gabe by her side should have comforted her but it only increased her gut-churning tension.

He was a man who'd never bend, never gentle to tenderness. Certainly not for his convenient bride. Instead, as his kisses had shown, he'd demand. And he'd demand far more than she'd ever expected to have to give.

"Do you, Jessica Bailey Randall, take this man to be your lawful wedded husband?"

And even then, something inside of her was waiting for Damon's familiar voice to call the wedding to a halt. If he had, she might have given up everything—her principles, her promises, her loyalties. But Damon didn't come, as he hadn't come yesterday, though everyone in Kowhai had to know she was back.

She set her jaw. "I do." Her eyes were locked with Gabe's as she spoke and she was startled by the open hunger that stirred in their depths, though she shouldn't have been. Gabriel Dumont was a man who held onto what he owned. Of course he'd be possessive with his bride, no matter that she'd been chosen for reasons other than passion.

As far as Gabe was concerned, she was now *his*.

She felt herself jerk at a loud cheer and realized she'd missed the rest of the ceremony.

"Jess?"

Blinking away her confusion, she looked up. "What?"

There was something very male in his eyes as he brushed aside a curl that had escaped her upswept hairdo. "They want a kiss. And so do I."

"Oh." She could feel a blush creeping over her cheeks as she stood on tiptoe, one hand braced against his shoulder.

When Gabe slid his palm across her bare nape, the roughness of his skin was an erotic caress she wasn't ready for. She tried to stifle her gasp, but he'd heard. Smiling with masculine approval, he pressed her close using his other hand on her lower back. And then he kissed her.

Possession. Absolute, undeniable possession.

That was what it felt like, a branding even more dangerous than the claim of his kiss the night before. Yet once again, she couldn't keep her body from molding to his, her arms from going around his waist, reason and sense obliterated under an avalanche of piercing sensation.

An unexpected wolf-whistle splintered the moment, jolting her into pulling away. But she only got loose because Gabe decided to set her free. In the second before he turned to face the others, she saw something both very satisfied and very impatient in his eyes.

Gabriel was ready to seal their deal.

In the most physical way.

Three

Four hours, endless dances with the station hands and two flutes of champagne later, Jess was having trouble deciding what to wear. Stripping down to the corset-like lace teddy, which was all she'd been able to find to support her under the smooth lines of the dress, was out of the question. So was the slinky nightgown gifted to her by a beaming Mrs. C.

But if she wore her favorite old T-shirt, Gabe might think she was being deliberately provocative, defying both him and the explicitly stated rules of their agreement. She had no doubts that he was ruthless enough to call off the whole cold-blooded affair if she didn't hold up her end of the bargain.

Which left her standing in front of the wardrobe, considering her options for the hundredth time. As a result, she was in no way prepared to hear the con-

NALINI SINGH   29

necting door between her room and the master
bedroom open.

Her heartbeat a jackhammer against her ribs, she
swiveled to face him. "I thought you were downstairs."

Having already undone and rolled up the cuffs to
bare sun-browned forearms, Gabe now undid the top
two buttons of his white dress shirt. "I figured my
business with Jim could wait."

"Oh." She lifted a hand to her hair then dropped it
again, not sure what to do with herself—knowledge was
one thing, experience quite another. "I'm not ready."

His smile was slow, sensual and very pleased. "I'll
take care of that."

She blushed despite having coached herself to be calm
and sensible about the whole thing. What she hadn't
factored in was the sheer impact of Gabriel Dumont.
And tonight, he was concentrating solely on her.

Her breath grew jagged and she found it difficult to
focus—her vision had constricted until the only thing
she could see was her new husband. Reaching her, he
put his hands on her waist, that smile segueing into an
expression that was darker, more sexual. Her body re-
sponded to the change with a melting warmth that
shocked her into an instant of clarity.

She raised her own hands and put them against his
chest with some vague idea of holding him off. She
realized her mistake immediately—the flimsy barrier
would do nothing to keep him at bay, not when her
body was all too willing. And as the heat of him
scorched her through the fine cotton of his shirt, she
found herself craving more rather than less.

Leaving one hand on her waist, he began to pull out

the pins in her hair with the other. "I like your curls, Jess." Stark masculine approval.

"It's become a lot more auburn since I was young." She didn't know why she'd made that inane comment. As if he cared that she'd been a real carrot-top until fate had taken pity on her. Even after having lost weight, she considered her hair her one glory…and Gabriel liked it. That shouldn't have mattered, but it did.

"Hmm." He continued to unravel the piled mass, dropping the pins to the floor. "I don't want you to cut it." She made a non-committal noise and he smiled, a gleam in his eye. "You wouldn't hack it off just to spite me, would you?"

The childish thought had, in fact, passed through her head a second before, but she wasn't going to admit that. Especially when she didn't understand it herself—it simply seemed to be wrong to *enjoy* any aspect of this marriage that had been meant to be the coldest of transactions. "Are the pins all out?"

He thrust both hands through the waves. "Looks like it." Prosaic words but his fingers were playing along the back of her nape, teasing the already sensitive spot.

She wanted to sigh and beg for more.

What was she thinking? Panic at her complete inability to remain strong against this man shot through her bloodstream, giving her courage a frantic boost. "Gabe, you don't have to go slow. Let's get this over with." It was a willful attempt to provoke him. An angry Gabriel would be far easier to resist than this temptingly seductive male with his ability to ignite things in her that should have been dead to him.

But his only reaction was to shake his head. "Oh, no,

Jess. You don't get to reduce this to nothing more than a quick, meaningless bang."

Embarrassment flooded her. But he wasn't finished. "I'm going to pleasure you, my *darling* wife. It's my job as your husband."

She was sure he was taunting her. "Stop playing games."

Moving so swiftly that she had no chance to step away, he scooped her up in his arms. "I'm absolutely serious. I want my wife screaming for me."

Her skin went taut at the utter resolve in those green eyes. She could find no words with which to respond as he carried her to the master bedroom and set her on her feet by the bed. The sexual charge between them was electric.

Caught in its surge, she didn't have the will to drop her arms from his neck as he wrapped his own around her back and began to slide down the zipper, slow and careful. Every nerve in her body was already stretched to the limit—the leisurely descent threatened to make them snap. Taking a shuddering breath, she closed her eyes in an effort to regain her balance.

His lips followed her into the darkness, sweeping her under. Gabriel kissed like the man he was—confident, possessive and fully in control. One of his hands rose to tangle in her hair, tugging back her head to facilitate his taking of her mouth, while the other slipped inside the now open zipper to lie flat on the naked skin of her upper back.

She moaned, captured by the undercurrent of hunger that lay every sweep of his tongue, every press of his lips. *Escape* was a word she no longer remembered and *addiction* was a very real possibility.

When he did set her free, it was only so he could kiss his way across her jaw and down her neck. She tipped her head, cooperating without conscious thought. Nothing she'd ever done had prepared her for this assault on her senses, this layering of pleasure upon pleasure.

Gabriel's hand was rough against her skin, the hand of a man who worked the land. But on her neck, his lips were almost velvet soft—a seductive contrast. She lost her breath as he closed his teeth over a pulse point, then released with exquisite deliberation, scraping those same strong teeth along the sensitive flesh.

"Mmm."

Her senses melted under the sound of blatant male appreciation. And the surrender was so sudden and total that something slumbering inside of her jerked to full wakefulness. This wasn't right, wasn't how it should be.

She'd prepared herself for going to bed with Gabriel, had told herself she'd *bear* the experience, though it would hurt to sleep with a man she didn't love. Yet here she was, coming apart in his arms. It confused her, made her want to pull away. But the fact was that her last-ditch effort to regain control stood no chance of success, she was so completely out of her league.

Under her dress, Gabe curved one hand around her ribs to lightly brush the side of a lace-covered breast, destroying all thoughts of rebellion. Her sharp cry made him chuckle. It was a very sexual sound. Even she understood that tone, the tone of a man who knew he had a woman in the palm of his hands. Tonight he was the master and she very much the novice.

The thought sparked a new burst of defiance. She might not be able to stop herself from going under but she refused to give in completely. Thrusting her hands into his hair, she tugged and made him raise his head. "Why do I have to be the one who's undressed first?" Her voice was husky, her words uttered on a gasp, but at least she'd gotten them out.

"Here I am. Unbutton the shirt." It was both an order and a dare. He didn't think she'd do it.

So she did.

Tanned male skin appeared bare inches from her lips— pure temptation that locked up her throat and shot arrows of need to her most private core. She'd made a bad miscalculation. However she had no intention of backing down. Mouth dry, she continued down his chest and stomach, pulling the shirt from his pants to finish the job.

When he kissed her again, her hands were still between their bodies and it was inevitable that she'd flatten them on his chest. The shock of skin to skin contact made her tremble. There was nothing soft about Gabriel. The man was built like a lean, beautiful machine and the womanly heart of her could only appreciate him.

When he slid the hand from her hair along her shoulders, she instinctively understood the silent request. Dropping her hands from his chest, she let him pull the dress down her arms. To her surprise, he stopped with the neckline just above her breasts and let go. Her hand shot up in a responsive movement, clutching the satin to her chest.

His eyes glittered with passion, unshielded in a way she'd never before seen. "Do it for me, Jess."

There was nothing else she could do, not with the fury of passion between them. Her body had triumphed over her mind, taken over everything she'd ever known about her own needs and desires. Unable to hold the power of that gaze, she looked away…and released the dress. It slid off her body like cool water.

Silence.

She found the courage to look up.

Green eyes clashed with her own and time stopped.

"Beautiful." He broke the connection to run those eyes down the corset-like teddy, to the point where the lace tops of her stockings met the bare skin of her upper thighs. Then he retraced his journey, leaving her scarcely able to breathe. And that was before he shrugged off his shirt.

She bit back a whimper but not soon enough.

"If you want to touch, do it." His hands went to her waist and stroked down to close over the curves of her bottom with boldness that made it very, very clear he considered her his in the most basic sense.

Hands fisted against his chest, she fought the urge to lean closer to taste him. His skin was beautiful, healthy and golden brown, radiating power. A second later, he used that strength to pick her up and drop her lightly on the bed.

Then never taking his eyes off her, he sat down on the edge to remove his socks. The muscled temptation of his back laid waste to her final defenses. She was about to reach out to touch when he stood. His hands went to his belt.

Fingers grasping the sheets, she watched mesmerized as he unbuckled the belt and pulled it out of the loops. It fell to the carpeted floor with a dull metallic sound. But she could hardly hear anything, her attention fixated on his fingers as they undid the top button of his pants.

Then he pulled down the zipper.

Cheeks ablaze, she closed her eyes and felt—more than heard—his low chuckle as he got rid of the pants and climbed into bed beside her. Throwing one leg over her lower body, he put a hand on her stomach. "I'm not naked…yet." It was a scandalous whisper in her ear.

Opening her eyes, she found his lips a thought away from hers, his eyes holding no amusement despite that chuckle. The hand on her stomach slid lower.

"Stay with me," he ordered when she would have turned her head.

She stayed, admitting to herself that she was a full participant in this dance at the very instant that he moved to cup her intimately. Her body arched up and she found herself squeezing her thighs to hold him to her. Giving a hoarse groan, he kissed her hard, that big hand rubbing the excruciating need between her legs. A second later, he was gone. She cried out at the loss, the sound so desperate she shocked herself.

"I want you naked." His fingers begin to unlace the ribbons holding together the teddy. His clenched jaw left no question as to the force of his arousal. "Where did you get this?"

"Hollywood Boulevard," she managed to answer.

Kissing the curve of her neck, he pushed one hair-roughened thigh between hers. "Wear it for me again." It was a definite command.

She might have protested his arrogance had he not chosen that moment to peel apart the sides of the teddy and cover a breast with his palm. Her mind splintering, she pushed into that callused male touch. But he released her far too soon. She had to bite her lower lip to keep from begging him to come back.

"I like the way you look at me, Jess. Now it's time for me to look at you." Rising to his knees, he moved until he could tug the teddy off completely and throw it

aside. Then he took inventory of her with his eyes—
from the tips of her stocking-covered toes to the curves
of her hips to the peaks of her breasts. Jess felt every
look like a physical touch and when he pushed up her
legs to bend them at the knee, she didn't have the will
to protest, much less the ability.

He spread her knees to kneel between them, his body
heat an exquisite caress. Running his hands under her
thighs and bottom to her lower back, he pulled her up
to straddle him.

"Oh!" She grabbed at his shoulders to steady herself,
suddenly conscious of the rigid length of his arousal
against her.

It was as if he'd seen the knowledge in her eyes.
"Relax, darling. I haven't finished tasting you."

She swallowed. In this position, she was completely
at his mercy. But he didn't tease, instead gave her
exactly what she wanted by dipping his head and taking
her nipple into his mouth. The hard suction tugged low
and deep inside of her, tempting her, taunting her.

Her fingernails dug into his shoulders, the flesh slick
and hot under her skin. He was so unapologetically
male that everything female in her reacted to him, soft-
ening, weakening…melting.

As a result, when he used his hands to ease her down
onto the bed, she was lost enough to say, "Gabe, *please.*"

Swearing under his breath, he moved to drag off his
briefs. But he returned to his position an instant later, his
hands going under her thighs. "Wrap your legs around
my waist." The rawness of his voice was as much an aph-
rodisiac as the skin stretched tight over his cheekbones.

She did as he asked. And realized that her body was
angled slightly upward, in perfect position for his

claiming. Instinct screamed that the penetration would be deep, incredibly so. "Gabe," she whispered. "It'll be too much."

"I'll ease you through it." He stroked his hand up her body to curve over her breast and though his words were calm, his eyes were anything but.

She had the feeling he was hanging on by a very thin thread, the pulsing length of his erection a physical mark of desire against the sensitive skin of her inner thigh. A small part of her feared the intensity of him, but that part was buried under the crushing force of her own need.

Gripping her bottom, he nudged at her with that length of hard, hot flesh. Lightning sizzled up her body and when he pushed in, she screamed. But Gabe was true to his word, easing his way into her so slowly she thought she'd go mad. He touched places inside of her that no one had ever touched, bringing intense pleasure.

And no pain.

"I'm damn glad you're a rider, Jess," he almost growled as he filled her, going so deep that she could feel his heartbeat in her body.

Not aware enough to understand what he was referring to, she squeezed intimate muscles around him in a reaction as old as time itself. Throwing back his head, he tightened his hold on her and began to move. His rhythm was fast, his strokes deep. She screamed and screamed as he pushed her over the edge in a tempest of hot breaths and powerful thrusts.

And when she fell, it was as a marked woman. Gabriel Dumont's woman.

Jess felt raw, exposed. He'd shattered her, claimed her passion and left her powerless. And she'd let him.

Begged him. Now that the haze of desire had faded to reveal harsh reality, she couldn't accept or understand the depth of her capitulation.

He wasn't supposed to be the man who made her yearn!

It felt as though she'd given up her dream in that bed…given up Damon. Every time she'd felt pleasure, every time she'd screamed, she'd betrayed the love that had lived in her heart for a lifetime. And she didn't understand how that could have happened. Gabe wasn't the kind of man she could ever love. She wasn't even sure she liked him.

Sliding quietly out of bed, she pulled on the first thing that came to hand. Unfortunately, it was Gabe's shirt. The scent of him was in the fibers, on her skin, in the air. It mocked her with echoes of what he'd taken…what she'd relinquished. As she searched for her dress so she could get rid of the shirt, she heard the sheets rustle.

"Where are you going, Jess?"

A bedside lamp came on.

Blinking against the glare, she tucked her hair behind her ears and buttoned up the shirt. "To my own bedroom."

His eyes were cold, focused. "I was under the impression you were already there."

"Look," she said, finding courage from the ragged tatters of her pride. "We've consummated the marriage. There's no need for us to be in the same bed anymore. I'd rather sleep on my own." She hugged her arms around herself. "I'll…I'll let you know if we were successful."

He raised an eyebrow. "I'm not that arrogant—it's probably going to take more than one try."

She bit her lower lip, trying not to look at the muscled upper body she'd caressed so feverishly less than an hour ago. "Well we can't do anything for a couple of days anyway. It didn't hurt during but I'm sore now." Despite the humiliating awkwardness of the admission, she forced herself to meet his eye, aware that Gabriel would capitalize on the slightest indication of weakness with brutal efficiency.

He flicked off the light. "Suit yourself. But don't try to use sex against me. I don't play those kinds of games."

"I'm not playing a game."

"Aren't you?" He snorted. "If you think I'm going to agree to carry on with a marriage where my wife saves herself for another man, you're sadly mistaken."

Four

"How dare you!"

"I asked you to be my wife, not my roommate. Decide what you want."

Not replying, Jess slammed through the connecting door between their rooms. Gabriel folded his arms behind his head and unclenched his jaw with conscious application of will. No woman had *ever* made the rules in his bed. And Jess wasn't going to get the chance to be the first. He'd meant what he'd said—he had no intention of living in a sexless marriage, not when bed was the one place where he… Shoving away that thought, he sat up.

Sleep was not what he wanted right now. He'd been more than ready for a replay of their first time together before Jess had pulled her little stunt. The woman had turned into pure lightning in his arms, the most responsive lover he'd ever had. He hadn't wanted passion when he'd chosen her, hadn't thought she'd incite it in him. But she had. He was willing to live with that fact, so long as it was confined to the bed. The primitive in him liked knowing he'd been the only man to taste his wife's screams.

Hard on the heels of that thought came a far less pleasant one. *Damon*. Gabriel had made it his business to keep tabs on the other man since learning of the separation and knew that he'd recently been sniffing around for information about Jess.

His hand fisted.

Jess could love Damon all she liked. It made no difference to Gabe except that it meant she'd never expect anything emotional from him. But he had no intention of putting up with a "friendship" between his wife and the younger man.

Jess might hate Gabe for it but she'd known who and what he was when she'd married him. He held on to what was his and Jess was now *his*. End of story.

Jess woke with gritty eyes. Checking the clock, she saw it was a few minutes before five. "Four hours of sleep. Great." A sound reached her from the bedroom next door and she realized Gabe was probably already up. Trying *not* to think about him or what they'd done in the tantalizing privacy of the night, she tugged the blanket to her chin.

The scent that rose up around her was that of the very man she'd been attempting to ignore. Thoughts derailed by anger, she'd forgotten to take off Gabe's shirt and now the lapse taunted her into full consciousness. "Arrgh!" She decided she might as well get up and shower.

The hot water poured a balm over muscles unused to

the kind of activity she'd indulged in the previous night. An activity she definitely did not want to think about, but which she couldn't seem to excise from her brain.

She'd just finished dressing and was standing in front of the window brushing her hair when a perfunctory knock sounded on the connecting door. Gabe walked in a second later. Clad in an old pair of jeans and a rough work shirt, his sexuality was somehow even more intense, more powerfully real. Her nerves quickfired, recalling the demands he'd made in the dark, the exquisite pain of sensual pleasure.

"Good morning." He gave her an amused smile, clearly aware of his effect on her.

That arrogance snapped her back to her senses. "I didn't say you could come in." Pulling the brush hard through her hair, she returned her attention to the predawn darkness.

He closed the gap to stand next to her, a powerful presence she'd touched intimately but knew only as a shadow. "Be ready to head out at seven."

"Where are we going?"

"To visit your parents."

Her animosity disappeared. "Thank you." Placing the brush on the windowsill, she forced herself to face him.

The eyes that looked back at her were completely unreadable. "Kiss me good morning, Jess."

"I don't take orders well."

"Funny, you followed them perfectly last night."

Her spine stiffened to ruler-straightness. "Exactly the kind of thing a woman wants to hear after her first time."

He winced. "Point taken."

Her mouth fell open at the oblique apology. Gabe took full advantage, sliding his hand to her nape and claiming the kiss he'd asked for. Still sensitive from the unbridled sexuality of the previous night, her defenses were pitifully weak. She was horrified to hear herself make a sound of protest when he began to pull away. But Gabe liked it. Folding her into his arms, he kissed her with even more intensity.

By the time he finally left the room, she was in complete emotional disarray. This had not been in the plan, this acute response to his touch. She'd always talked about love and sex in the same breath, always assumed she'd care deeply for any man she made love with. Yet here she was, shattering every time Gabe touched her. It shamed her deeply.

And the worst thing was, she had no idea how to fight it. Her love for Damon had insulated her against other men since the day she'd reached adulthood. But that shield had buckled under the potent seduction of Gabe's masculinity.

Unable to think of anything that would make her feel better about her sudden descent into lust unaccompanied by love or romance, she did what she always did when she needed to think. She pulled out a sketch pad and began to draw.

She began every project with a detailed sketch, never putting oil paint to canvas until she'd worked out all the dimensions and angles. In truth, she wasn't impulsive in any area of her art—she carefully thought through the subject before she created, step by slow step. But today she let her hand run free with no conscious interference. What emerged was an image of the face she'd carried in her heart for over a decade.

If only Damon hadn't waited so long to make that drunken call, she wouldn't be here. They would have been married long before her father's death, would have found some other way to hold onto Randall Station. But he'd waited until it was eons too late, Kayla's pregnancy combined with Jess's debt to Gabriel opening an impassable chasm between them.

That distance *hurt*. Damon had been her closest friend since childhood, their relationship a combination of mischief and laughter. He'd helped her see the sunshine again after her mother's early death, teasing her out of tears and forcing her to rejoin the world. She'd confessed her secrets to him, listened to his in return, and somewhere between childhood and womanhood, she'd fallen in love.

He'd broken her heart when he'd married Kayla. And he'd crushed it again with that phone call. "Why?" she whispered to the sketch. "Why did you wait so long?"

It was as well they hadn't met before her wedding— Jess wasn't sure she could have withstood his declarations in person. And now she was Gabriel's. Not that it mattered. If Damon had truly meant what he'd said, he would have tracked her down the moment she arrived home. But he hadn't. *Why?*

Throwing the pencil to the floor, she dropped her head into her hands. *"Help me."* It was a tortured whisper. But no one was listening.

Several hours later, Jess looked out at the Dumont family plot from inside the Jeep. She'd forced this visit but now that they were here, she was no longer sure she'd made the right decision. It was apparent that Gabe would much rather be elsewhere.

"Are you coming?" she asked, opening her door. He'd surprised her by accompanying her to her parents' graves. She had no idea what to expect from him this time, especially since he'd been so silent on the long drive back to Angel.

He undid his seat belt and got out, not saying a word as she opened the back door and reached for the greenery and flowers she'd gathered from around the station. But he was by her side when she walked toward the final resting places of Stephen, Mary, Raphael, Michael and Angelica Dumont.

Stopping in front of Raphael's grave, she looked up at him. "Would you like to lay the flowers?"

"No." His tone made it crystal clear he considered this a waste of time.

She was cut to the quick but refused to rush. This was important.

Gabe reacted only when she went to put flowers on his mother's resting place. Striding over, he moved them to his sister's instead.

"Gabe?"

"Are you done?"

"Yes." She rose from her crouch, eyes on the harsh lines of a face she found impossible to read. "But..."

"But what, Jess? They're dead and have been for twenty-five years." He glanced at his watch. "I have to check some fencing. We'd better head back."

She grabbed his hand to stop him when he would have turned away, acting more out of instinct than logic. His eyes slammed into hers, but she found the courage to stand her ground. "I'm sorry, I didn't realize how much this would hurt you."

He raised an eyebrow. "I'm fine. You're the one who wanted to come out here."

"Gabe," she began, convinced she'd glimpsed a deep

vulnerability behind his uncaring mask. Hope foun-
tained in her blood. Perhaps her marriage wouldn't be
a soulless one after all. If Gabe could feel so intensely,
then maybe what had gone on between them last night
hadn't been based on lust alone.

"Jess, you know me. I'm not some wounded hero you
have to save. I was ten years old when they died. I barely
remember them." Turning, he shrugged off her hand
and strode to the car.

Jess wanted to believe he was lying but the look on his
face as he'd spoken had been nothing but calm, nothing
but completely in control. Hope crumbled. No wonder
Gabe never visited his parents' and siblings' graves—the
man didn't even have the heart to love their memory.

An entire day and a surprisingly undisturbed night of
sleep later, Jess was sketching on the verandah when a
battered old pickup roared down the drive. She waited
for whoever it was to park and walk over, but the driver
raced all the way to the edge of the verandah before
braking to a sudden halt on the grass.

Frowning at the theatrics, she put down the sketch
pad. Who in the—? The vehicle's door swung open and
out jumped the last person she'd expected to see.

"Jessie girl!" Running up the steps, Damon wrapped
his arms around her waist and lifted her off her feet.

It was impossible not to be happy to see him, not when
she'd missed him so very much. Blue-eyed with jet black
hair, Damon had the looks of a movie star or a playboy.
But it was his smile she'd fallen for, a bright slash that
constantly proclaimed his amusement at the whole world.

She laughed for the first time since arriving back in
the country. "Let me down, you idiot."

That familiar smile faded. "I don't ever want to let you go." But he lowered her until her feet touched the floorboards. "Couldn't you have waited till I got back?" It was a pained accusation. "You didn't even give me a chance."

Butterflies in her stomach. The bad kind. "What?"

"I heard you got hitched while I was out of town."

"You heard right." Said in a quiet but lethal voice, the statement came from the other side of the verandah. "So I suggest you get your hands off her."

Aware how it must look, Jess moved out of Damon's arms, face flushing alternately hot and cold. "Damon came to say hello."

Gabe walked over to put his own arm around her waist. Rebelling against the display of ownership, she tried to pull away but unlike Damon, Gabe wasn't willing to budge. "Did he?"

Jess was surprised to see Damon's eyes narrow. "Did you even tell Jess I wanted to speak to her when she got back?" His chin jutted out.

"Funny," Gabe said, his tone completely reasonable and indefinably dangerous at the same time, "I thought they had phones all over the country."

Jess was starting to be scared for Damon. He was strong but no match for Gabe. She pleaded silently with him when he glanced at her and to her relief, his next words were civil. "I think me and Jessie need to talk."

Gabriel's arm became a steel trap. "You want to talk to my wife, you can do it right now."

"Yeah, sure. Later, Jess." Damon left with the same turbulence with which he'd arrived.

Jess didn't speak again until his pickup was a blur in the distance. Then she wrenched herself out of Gabe's hold to face him, arms crossed. "What did you think you were doing?"

"I thought I was making it clear that you're now my wife, something you seemed to have forgotten." His eyes glittered with anger. "How long were you planning to make out with him in front of half the station?"

Fury prompted her reply. "He's been my friend for almost as long as I've been alive. Did it occur to you that maybe he wanted to talk to me about what's going on in his life?" She pushed aside the memory of Damon saying he never wanted to let her go, because that *did* make her feel guilty.

"I don't care what the hell he wanted to talk about." Gabe folded his own arms, a solid wall of dominance. "There'll be no more private chats between the two of you."

"You're my husband, not my keeper!"

"I shouldn't need to be your keeper. Or do you think it's perfectly acceptable to throw yourself into the arms of your would-be lover?"

"You're twisting everything around!" When she'd hugged Damon, it had been out of the most innocent kind of happiness. But Gabe was making it sound sordid, making her question her every action, her every word.

His jaw was granite, his next statement icy cold. "I swear to God, Jess, if you try to cheat on me with that useless excuse for a man, I'll divorce you so fast your head will spin. And then I'll accept the developers' offer—they haven't lost interest."

She felt the blood leach out from under her skin. "You wouldn't." Even Gabe wouldn't be so cruel. "I've given you *everything*."

He scoffed. "You signed on for life, not one quick

tumble in my bed. If that was what I'd wanted, I could've gotten it much cheaper and from someone far more experienced than you, sweetheart."

The verbal slap hit so hard she couldn't find her voice.

"Your land has no real value to me in terms of this operation," he continued. "I bought it to seal our deal and I can get rid of it as easily if you can't do your job as my wife. Think about that the next time you have an urge to meet your *friend*." He left without giving her the chance to reply. Though what she would have said, she didn't know.

Collapsing into the chair, she cradled her head in her hands. But that didn't stop her mind from spinning into chaos. Gabe's threat had shocked her, making it viciously clear that her new husband trusted her about as much as he'd trust an alley cat. Still, she couldn't believe he'd taunted her with what he knew to be her greatest vulnerability.

The idea of her parents' legacy being razed for what the developers had called a retreat for the rich and famous, complete with swimming pool, tennis courts and a golf course, was her personal nightmare. They would destroy the beauty of everything her parents had worked so hard to achieve, an insult to their memory she simply couldn't bear. Unlike Gabriel, she cherished those memories. They were all she had left.

"Jess?"

Mrs. Croft's voice startled her into dropping her hands. "What is it?"

The older woman took in Jess's expression with concerned eyes but didn't ask any questions. "You've got a call." She handed over the portable phone.

"Thanks." Jess was about to answer when Mrs. C.

made a gesture that had her placing a hand over the mouthpiece.

"You made your choice when you said your vows, my girl. Don't be looking back now." With that advice, the other woman walked back inside the house.

Defeated by this evidence of yet another person who found it easy to believe she'd be unfaithful, Jess said a quiet, "Hello."

"You alone, Jessie?"

Five

Her hand froze around the receiver. "Do you have a death wish, Damon? If Gabe had picked up the phone—"

"I would have hung up. No big deal." He laughed but there was a bitter undertone to it she'd never before heard from him.

"Why are you calling?"

"I told you I wanted to talk to you." A small pause. "You're still my friend, aren't you?"

Her heart softened. "Of course I am."

"Even if he says no?"

"Don't go there." Gabriel was the one topic she'd never discuss with Damon. "What's this I'm hearing about you and Kayla?" she asked instead, trying to be his friend.

The pause was longer this time. "We're done. I told you I should've never married her in the first place."

"Damon," she began, but he was already speaking.

"*I told you* and you went ahead and married that bast—" He cut himself off before she could. "I don't love her anymore."

"You don't mean that." And yet part of her, a part she didn't particularly like, hoped that he did. She'd held that secret hope ever since Kayla's car had broken down in Kowhai two years ago, and the beautiful brunette and Damon had become a couple almost overnight.

"You know who I should've married, don't you?" His voice lowered, became huskier.

She should have disconnected then and there but she didn't, overwhelmed by a need that had been years in the making. Because even in that single long-distance phone call, he hadn't said what she most needed to hear.

What she couldn't even let herself think, much less admit, was that she was acting this way out of anger at Gabriel.

"You, Jess. I should've married you."

She pressed the end button with fingers that wouldn't stop trembling. She hated herself for having allowed Damon to go on, loathed the need in her that had turned her into the worst kind of hypocrite. Because while she might not have crossed the physical line into disloyalty, she'd inarguably crossed an emotional one.

The phone jangled to life again so suddenly she almost dropped it. "Hello?" A wary question.

The caller turned out to be Merri Tanner, a neighbor. Relieved, Jess chatted with her for a minute or two before Merri said, "We're having a bit of a barbecue tonight if you feel up to coming. Around sevenish. It's a busy time but we figured folks could use the chance to blow off some steam."

A social buffer between her and Gabe was precisely what she needed today. "Sure. Sounds fun." Hanging up after another few minutes, she stared out at the land in front of her. So strong, so enduring and capable of causing such pain to the human heart.

Tempting as it was to ask someone else to take a message about the barbecue to Gabe, that would have been cowardly. And her self-respect had already plunged to new depths after Damon's call. Putting the phone on the chair, she went to find her husband.

When guilt threatened to deprive her of her confidence, she fought it by nurturing her anger at Gabe's cruel threat, refining it, making it razor sharp. She would not give Gabriel Dumont the chance to use that indomitable will of his to crush her.

She located him talking to the foreman. He broke off his conversation when she caught his eye. "What is it?" There was no trace of anger in his voice. There was, in fact, no trace of any emotion.

"Merri's invited us over for a barbecue. Around seven." She folded her arms. "I said we'd come."

"Fine." He reached out to tap her cheek with his index finger and the touch was so unexpectedly gentle, she didn't know how to react. "Must've been a long phone call—your skin's red here."

Jerking away, she wondered if he could read the guilt in her eyes. Because this time, she *had* done something she wasn't proud of. But even that didn't excuse the things he'd said to her and she wasn't going to pretend otherwise. "Drop the act, Gabe. You feel more tenderness toward your bank balance than toward me."

Something changed in his expression, became harder. "Good thing isn't it? If I didn't have that bank balance, you'd have been left high and dry." Giving her a grim smile, he went back to his interrupted conversation with Jim.

Jess grit her teeth and told herself not to care. Easier said than done. The fact that he was right just rubbed salt into her wounds. She was no gold-digger but she'd needed what Gabe's money could do. If money hadn't been a factor, she'd never have made this devil's bargain. But she had. And now she had to pay the price.

Leaving the barn before she said something she shouldn't, she headed to the house and decided to make a salad for the barbecue. Since the food preparation distracted her, at least for a little while, she baked a marble cake as well.

By the time five-thirty rolled around, everything was ready to go and so was she. She'd chosen her clothes with care, needing to feel good about herself—a calf-length wool skirt and white angora sweater teamed with her favorite knee-high leather boots.

Gabe hadn't said a word upon entering the kitchen, where she was putting everything into a picnic basket. But now he fingered the damp strands of her hair. "I think I'll get you to leave the boots on tonight."

She knew he was being deliberately provocative in response to her cool attitude, but her treacherous body wanted to shiver at the implied eroticism. Pulling away, she put several feet of distance between them.

"Cat got your tongue, Jess?" Wearing sand-colored corduroy trousers and a cable-knit sweater in dark navy, he looked both confident and intrinsically male. "Want me to find it for you?"

Ignoring the taunt, she picked up the basket. "Let's head off."

Gabe reached out and took the basket from her. She didn't fight him, able to tell that it had been an instinctive act on his part. If she made a fuss, he'd figure out pretty damn quick that she was nowhere near as calm as she was attempting to appear.

"It'll take us more than two hours to drive over to their spread. I'll fly us instead."

"No. I want to drive." It was an impulsive decision— she needed the solid earth beneath her feet.

Raising an eyebrow, he nonetheless walked out to the rugged Jeep he'd parked in front of the house. "Fine." He put the basket in back.

Opening the passenger door, she started to get in. "Merri said sevenish so that probably means it'll be close to eight by the time most folks make it anyway."

Gabe grabbed her door when she would have pulled it shut. The scent of his aftershave wove around her like a net. "Try not to glare at me all evening. It's hardly the impression I want to give people of our marriage." Slamming the door, he walked around to the driver's side and got in.

"If you're going to blackmail me with the developers' offer, then don't expect me to be sweetness and light."

"Sweetness and light?" He snorted and started the car. "Jessie, you've been sulking since you landed."

"Don't call me that."

The tires squealed as he accelerated down the drive. "Why? Because it's Damon's pet name for you?"

"That has nothing to do with it."

"Could've fooled me."

She folded her arms. "People who like me use that name. You don't like or trust me. So stick with Jess or Jessica."

He didn't say a word for the next two hours and neither did she. It was only as they were about to pull into the Tanners' place that she broke their silence. "Is there any other news I should know?"

"You know the biggest." He brought the Jeep to a smooth stop behind a mud-splattered small truck. Contrary to Jess's prediction, it looked as though a lot of people had already arrived. "You've probably heard that Sylvie's back from the States."

Ice shot through her veins. "When did that happen?"

"Couple of months ago." Nothing in his tone betrayed his feelings on the subject, leaving her at the mercy of her own imagination. The rumor was that Sylvie had broken off her relationship with Gabe in order to pursue her career.

If the gossip was true, then Jess could well believe Gabe would refuse to forgive Sylvie, even going so far as to marry another woman. But that didn't mean he no longer had feelings for the beautiful blonde...feelings he'd never have for his bride. Not that she cared. Jess shoved open her door with enough force to send it swinging.

Grabbing the basket, they walked toward the Tanners' large backyard side by side. Halfway there Gabe put his arm around her and bent so close his breath fanned her hair as he spoke. "Smile, Jessica. We're supposed to be in the honeymoon phase."

She didn't know what made her do it. Sliding her own arm around his waist, she gave him a saccharine sweet smile as they rounded the final corner. "Oh *honey*, that's so sweet!"

Gabe's low warning came too late. Several people had overheard and were now ribbing him about turning soft. He took the kidding good-naturedly, but his arm didn't move from around her waist, even as he handed over the basket to young Simon Tanner.

Jess used the excuse of shaking Mr. Tanner's hand to withdraw her own arm from around Gabe's waist. It made her feel decidedly odd to sense the warmth of him through their clothing, an intimacy so quiet it was more disturbing than if they'd been exchanging passionate kisses.

"Good to see you, Jess," Mr. Tanner boomed. "We missed you."

"It's nice to be home."

"Gabriel, you've done well. Jess is the prettiest girl here."

"I know."

Jess had to fight the urge to kick Gabe for that bold-faced lie. She thought she'd glimpsed Sylvie Ryan's stunning form in the glow of the fairy lights and hurricane lanterns that had been strung out over the yard.

"Good, good." Mr. Tanner saw someone else arriving and went off to welcome them, leaving Gabe and Jess to be congratulated by a steady stream of well-wishers.

"Thank you," she said for the fiftieth time and made an unobtrusive move to pull away from the disconcerting heat of Gabe's touch. His arm tightened. Unable to say anything because of the others, she smiled and kept up the chatter, all the while wondering if the man was ever going to let her go.

"So when are you two giving a party to celebrate the wedding?" Kerry Lynn asked Jess, while her husband spoke with Gabe.

"We haven't discussed it."

"Well, sometime soon would be good you know. Wait much longer and work's going to hit fever pitch."

Jess nodded. Most of the people in this area owned or worked for stations. "What kind of a party would you suggest?" Her question was more for conversation's sake than because she really wanted an event to celebrate the mockery of her marriage.

"A sit-down dinner would be nice. Like in a reception hall."

Jess couldn't think of anything worse than being stuck in front of people scrutinizing her and Gabe's every move. "Or maybe an upscale-type picnic," she threw out in desperation. "We could get it catered, have tables and chairs out on the lawn, some music so people could dance."

"That sounds wonderful, darling," Gabriel said, and she knew he was laughing at her. "If we set up a marquee and put out some space-heaters, it shouldn't be too cold."

"Uh-huh," she muttered, hoping that that would be the end of it.

"Oh, Graham's band could play!" Kerry clapped her hands, drawing another group to theirs.

Several people seconded her suggestion and Graham Lynn beamed. Jess had the sense of control slipping through her fingertips. "I didn't know you had a band, Graham," she said weakly, leaning against Gabe without conscious thought.

He hugged her to his side and took charge of the conversation with a disarming charm she'd never have expected from him. "We'll let you know soon as we have a date. But for now, we'd better go say hello to some of the others before Jess's jet lag catches up with her."

The group smiled and let them escape but Jess knew the deal was done. "We're going to have to hold that damn party aren't we?"

"Tut-tut, such language, Jessica."

"Stop calling me Jessica." She knew it was a stupid response when she was the one who'd told him to use that name, but it sounded completely wrong. "No one calls me that."

"Your husband does, Jessica darling." His lips brushed her ear as he spoke.

She was fighting a losing battle against the butterflies in her stomach when a husky female chuckle broke the moment. "Well, well, if it isn't Mr. and Mrs. Dumont."

Steeling her spine, Jess looked up. "Hello, Sylvie. Gabriel said you were back."

"Hi, sweetie." Sylvie leaned in to kiss Jess on the cheek as if they were old friends. The truth was the exact opposite—the daughter of a judge and a large station owner, Sylvie Ryan had never before deigned to speak to a nobody like Jess Randall.

Feeling dwarfed by the model-height woman, Jess grit her teeth and smiled. Gabe chose that moment to finally release her. "I've been wanting to speak to Derek about something," he said, jerking his head at the pilot standing near the food table. "Nice to see you again, Sylvie."

"Likewise." Sylvie's tone held an insinuation Jess told herself to ignore. However, she could hardly overlook the fact that the other woman had all but announced that she and Gabe had once been lovers.

"You married, Sylvie?" she asked after Gabe was out of earshot. The jab was petty of her but she wasn't feeling particularly mature right then.

Sylvie's smile slipped a fraction. "You seem to have snapped up the only man worth anything around here."

"Lucky me."

"The true test is whether you can hold him."

Six

And the claws were out. "I guess you'd know from experience." Jess made her smile so sweet, Sylvie clearly had no idea whether she'd been insulted or not. "Oh, look, I see Merri over there. You'll have to excuse me, I haven't had a chance to speak to her."

Glad to be out of range of the other woman's honey-laced barbs, Jess located a couple of chairs and got some food before sitting down with Merri for a good chat.

"You'd better keep an eye on that one," her friend said twenty minutes later, as they were about to dig into a shared slice of chocolate cake.

Jess followed Merri's gaze in time to see Sylvie put a hand on Gabe's shoulder and press close to whisper in his ear. When he smiled, something new and unexpected inside of Jess, twisted. She stabbed at the cake with unnecessary force. "She hasn't changed a bit."

"Uh-uh." Merri swallowed a bite. "She went after Gabe like a freight train as soon as she got back. I heard she was up at Angel most every day before you arrived."

The chocolate cake was a dry husk in her throat. "Oh."

"But he married you, so I don't think you have anything to worry about." Merri's grin was gleeful. "Must make Queen Sylvie want to spit."

Jess wasn't so sure she *had* won. Gabe and Sylvie looked very comfortable with each other as they stood talking. Height, looks, social standing, they were equals in all that and more. Maybe the real reason Gabe hadn't married Sylvie was that the other woman made him feel emotions he'd rather not have in his life. Made him feel love.

"What's Sylvie do now?" Jess asked, wondering why she cared about Gabe's feelings for the blonde. It was hardly as if she herself loved him. But she was beginning to understand why he'd reacted so furiously to her jumping into Damon's arms this morning. If he'd done something similar with Sylvie…

"I hear she's taken a year's leave from some high-powered job with an international banking firm," Merri said, interrupting Jess's uncomfortable thoughts. "Maybe she thought she'd return and make up with Gabe." The other woman gasped. "Oh, Lord, she came. Did anyone tell you what's happened?"

Jess glanced over her shoulder at the absolute worst moment. Kayla's eye caught hers and the brunette began to walk over. Pregnancy had made Damon's wife more beautiful, her cheeks flushed with health, her hair a shiny mahogany that flowed down her back. But when she levered herself into a chair facing Jess and Merri, Jess saw the new lines of strain around her mouth.

"Hi, Jess. Mrs. C. mentioned you were back."

"Hi. Kayla." She didn't know what else to say and was waiting for Merri to save the moment when the other woman jumped to her feet.

"Mom's calling me. Back in a tick."

Grimacing inwardly at the ill-timed summons, Jess searched for a safe topic of conversation. But the single thing she and Kayla had in common was the one thing they couldn't talk about. "I'm sorry," Jess finally said, her confusion even greater than it had been this morning. Because not only was she truly sorry for Kayla, she was angry at Damon for creating this mess in the first place. "Gabe told me…."

Kayla tried to smile but couldn't quite pull it off. "It's hardly a secret."

"So, how far along are you?"

"Eight months." Biting her lower lip, the brunette put a hand on her rounded abdomen. "I wanted to ask you something."

Nervous tension was a rock in Jess's stomach. "What?"

"Damon…he listens to you. Could you—?" Kayla swallowed, obviously battling tears. "I don't even know what I want you to do. It's not as if you can get my husband to love me again."

Unable to sit silent in the face of such anguish, Jess put a hand over Kayla's. "I'll talk to him." An offer made from the soft heart that had already caused her so much pain.

"Th-thank you." Kayla took several deep breaths and seemed to be on the verge of recovery when her expression suddenly clouded over.

Jess only had to look across the lawn to find the reason why. Damon had arrived and joined in a laughing conversation with several others…until he spied her and Kayla. His face undergoing a sea change, he left the group to head in their direction.

"Go," Kayla whispered. "Jess, please stop him. I can't talk to him right now. I don't want everyone to see me cry." Her voice broke.

It would have taken a harder heart than Jess's to have refused. "Okay."

She could almost feel her husband's eyes on her as she covered the distance to Damon. That merely made her more determined. She had no intention of re-enacting this morning's mistake, but if Gabe thought she was going to come to heel like one of the station dogs, he had another think coming.

Then Damon threw his arms around her.

She'd had more than enough of male stupidity. "Let me go right this instant." This little display would likely both worsen things in her own marriage *and* cause Kayla considerable pain. Jess couldn't understand Damon's behavior—the boy she'd grown up with had never been vindictive or malicious.

He released her but she knew the damage had been done. "Can't I hug my best friend now?"

Well aware that his act had brought all eyes on them, she lowered her voice. "Don't play games. Kayla—"

"No, Jess. I don't want to talk about her." The stubborn set of his jaw was intimately familiar.

"Why not?" she pushed. "You always told me everything." Even his joy at first realizing he loved Kayla. "How could you do this, Damon? She's pregnant." Seeing Kayla had made at least one thing certain in Jess's mind— no matter what else, Damon had taken vows. He'd made promises. And Jess believed in keeping promises. Even if they hurt. Even if you changed your mind.

"Would it have been better if I'd stayed with her when I don't love her anymore?" he snapped, unknowingly rejecting the principles by which she lived her life. "I'm giving her our place and I'm going to support her and the baby, too, so don't make me into some kind of bad guy!" His voice dropped to a harsh whisper. "Don't be like the rest of them and judge me without knowing the facts. Not you too, Jess."

She thrust a hand through her hair, her mind going in a hundred different directions. Part of her despised Damon for what he'd done, and that was the one thing she couldn't have predicted. However, another part of her admired him for being true to his heart. Was she really making the better choice by remaining locked in a loveless marriage? "But—"

"I told you I love *you*," he interrupted, raising a hand as if to put it on her cheek. "I was just too stupid to realize it before."

Jess didn't know how she knew that Gabe had walked up behind her. She was praying her instincts were wrong when a muscled arm slid around her waist. All the blood left her face. "Gabe," she said, wanting to head off a confrontation.

"Be quiet, Jess." The order was so low she barely caught it, but the anger behind it made her want to shiver. "I told you to stay away from my wife."

"It's a free country."

"*Damon*." Jess shook her head at the younger man. After a taut second that threatened to end in violence, he gave a shrug and walked off to join the Johnson girls.

"Look at me and smile." It was a command she normally would have resisted but she had a feeling she'd already pushed Gabe to the limit.

Turning, she put a hand on his upper arm and looked up. "Whatever you think you heard, it wasn't what you thought."

He bent down to whisper in her ear and she knew it was a move calculated to give the impression of their being a loving couple. "Yeah? I thought I heard another man professing his love for you."

She felt her spine lock as he confirmed the worst-case scenario.

"Nothing to say?" He dropped a kiss on her cheek as he lifted his head.

"Don't—"

"We'll discuss it at home."

The night drive back to Angel was the worst of her life. Gabe didn't say a word and she knew it would be futile to try to make him talk when he'd decided otherwise. Even once they reached the station there was no respite—he left her to check on something Jim had called him about earlier.

By the time she heard him return to the master bedroom, she was a bundle of nerves. She wanted this confrontation over with, even if that meant she had to jump deliberately into the flames. Belting her dressing gown tightly closed over the camisole and pajama bottoms she wore, she knocked on the connecting door. There was no answer but she stepped through anyway.

Gabe sat on the edge of the bed, having already removed his sweater and T-shirt. Now, he dropped his balled-up socks to the floor and stood. "So eager to get to bed?" Holding her gaze, he undid his belt and pulled it out of the loops.

Her eye followed its descent to the floor. "Stop it,

Gabe," she said, nerves tingling with the awareness that her husband was in a very dangerous mood. "You know why I'm here."

He closed the distance between them, big and male with a glitter in his eyes that was pure anger. "Have you come to kiss and make up?"

She put up a hand to stop him but he walked into it, pressing her palm against his chest and holding it there with one of his own hands. The energy radiating from him burned through her skin and caressed things low and newly awakened.

She fought back, determined to conquer her body's hunger for this man she barely knew. "I came to talk."

"Talking is not what we do best, darling." In those angry eyes, she saw memories of their first night in this bed, sultry and dark, passionate and furious.

Her heart began to thud in anticipation and she hated herself for it. "Maybe we'd better start getting good at it." She broke his hold, surprised when he let her go.

"Why?" Reaching out, he thrust one of his hands into her hair, recapturing her. "I didn't marry you for conversation. I married you to get a well-behaved, undemanding and faithful wife who'd give me children. That you're hot in bed is a very nice bonus but the last I heard, having sex doesn't require talking."

She slapped him. "Damn you!"

His reaction was a smile that was anything but amused. "I was damned long ago, Jess. Don't you know what they say—Gabriel Dumont survived the fire because he made a deal with the devil."

"You're no devil, just a bastard."

"On the contrary my dear, my parents were very married." Thrusting his other hand into her hair, he pulled her close. His next words were spoken against her lips. "They used to talk but that didn't fix anything."

Something about that last statement struck Jess as indefinably wrong. Yet he gave her no chance to follow up, ending all conversation with a kiss that robbed her of both her breath and her sanity. Already in the grip of the passion of anger, she ignited at his first touch. Logic and reason flew out the window.

Her robe was on the floor two seconds later, Gabe's hands shoving under her camisole to lie flat against her back. Fueled by the rawest, most primitive of desires, she gripped his hair and took another kiss, giving back as good as she got. He made a harsh sound low in his throat and broke the kiss to run his hands down to her waistband.

Her panties and pajama bottoms joined the robe before she could do much more than gasp. Sucking in a shocked breath, she tried to say something—what, she didn't know—as he lifted her clear. But the sound was lost in the tumult of his next kiss and so was her mind.

When he tore away his lips to turn her so she faced the bed, she didn't understand what was happening…until she felt the hardness of him pressing against her through the closed zipper of his pants.

"Do it!" The order was guttural.

But that same unfamiliar wildness in her, the one that had reacted so explosively to his kiss, understood. It was an understanding of the body, not the mind—her thoughts were fragmented, her skin tight enough to hurt. Bending, she closed her hands around the thick wood of the bedpost.

And then she heard the zipper being lowered.

Even that warning wasn't enough. She screamed as

he pushed into her. Hard. Fast. Deep. Her body accepted him, welcomed his driving thrusts, but he was merciless in the intensity of what he asked of her, pushing her so far that she lost all traces of civilization and surrendered to her most primal heart.

Lying in the darkness, Jess didn't know who she was anymore—not only had she let Gabe love her with an intimacy that made her a traitor to her own emotions, she hadn't managed to make him talk about anything. Taking a deep breath, she moved to push off the sheets.

A strong arm clamped around her waist. "No, Jess. Tonight you stay with your husband."

When she opened her mouth to argue, he covered it with his own. There was no tenderness in his touch—it was a brand, a mark of possession. She tried to stifle her reactions, tried to regain command of a body that no longer seemed her own, but still she broke. Over and over and over.

And that was how she spent her nights for the next seven days. In Gabriel's bed, in Gabriel's arms, as he taught her that no matter how well she thought she knew herself, she knew nothing. In those dark hours, she discovered a hidden, deeply sensual part of herself that gloried in what went on between the sheets, an houri who cared for pleasure alone.

Yet even as he stripped her of her defenses, he maintained his own steely control. That was what hurt and frustrated her the most—Gabe had brought passion into a relationship she'd once believed would be pure business, made her want things she'd never have dreamed of at the start, but the passion was all on his terms.

The days weren't much better. She spent them tormented by memories of the nights, confusion a churning knot in her stomach. So when her paintings arrived, she was more than ready to do something, anything, to temper her descent into emotional chaos.

Ripping open the boxes, she began stacking the canvasses in the large ground-floor room she'd commandeered as her studio. "I'm good at this," she told herself, determined to rebuild her fractured confidence. She wasn't merely Gabriel Dumont's convenient wife, not merely the possession of a man who'd pushed her firmly to the periphery of his life—her place was in his bed and occasionally on his arm. Other than that, he didn't want to know him.

And she was finding the cold distance…hard.

Jess buried that thought soon as it rose. She'd entered this marriage knowing the rules. If she'd come to hope for more, then that was her mistake and one she'd be better off nipping in the bud.

Taking a calming breath, she set a prepared canvas on the easel she'd placed opposite the door, and picked up a soft pencil. Damon's face was easy for her to draw. She'd spent years staring at it with adoring eyes. But today, she saw things in it she'd never before seen…things that troubled her.

"Call for you, Jess, my girl."

She looked up with a start, not having heard it ring. "Who is it?"

"A Richard Dusevic."

Jess's eyes widened but she waited until Mrs. C. had left, to answer. "Mr. Dusevic?"

"Ms. Randall, I have on my desk several high-definition images my assistant tells me are of your work."

"Oh." *Very intelligent, Jess.*

"Can you send me the originals?"

Sounding calm became a test. "Sure. Would you like just the ones for which I submitted slides?"

"Give me a selection of your choice. I want to see what you can do. I have a feeling I won't be disappointed."

She crushed the receiver to her ear. "I'll get them couriered up to you A.S.A.P."

"I'll call you after I've had a chance to review them."

Jess nodded though he couldn't see her. "Thank you."

"Don't keep me waiting, darling." With that flamboyant goodbye, he hung up.

She put down the receiver and tried to breathe but that was pretty much impossible. "Oh my God, Richard Dusevic called me."

"How many men do you have, Jess?" The sardonic question came from the doorway.

Seven

Reacting out of instinct, she flicked a coversheet over her work-in-progress and smiled. Nothing could spoil her mood today. "Richard Dusevic is the owner of one of the most prestigious art galleries in New Zealand."

Gabe folded his arms and leaned against the door-jamb. "Congratulations."

"It's only a request to see work, not an offer," she clarified.

"But Dusevic doesn't go around asking everyone I gather?"

"No." She grinned and did a little dance. "I have to go to the post office tomorrow morning to send some paintings to Auckland. Can I borrow the SUV?"

"I'll drive you," he offered unexpectedly, a smile on his lips that actually reached his eyes. "I have to see someone there anyway."

She began to search through her work, disquieted by the happiness she felt at having made him smile.

"Are you going to show me your paintings?"

Surprised, she glanced at him. "Why should I?" It came out without thought, a snippy comment she hadn't known she had the capacity to make. "We don't talk, remember?"

"Been waiting to say that, haven't you?" He pulled up his body, his jaw an unyielding line.

Ashamed at having sunk that low, she shrugged and resumed her sorting. "I have work to do."

When she looked up a minute later, he was gone.

Giving a frustrated sigh, she sat on the floor, her head in her hands. Why had she done that? It would have made far more sense to have acted civilly and broken the ice between them. But she hated the idea of being what he'd described her as—*well-behaved, undemanding.*

She wasn't a pet or a child. And Gabriel Dumont was going to learn that while he might be able to enslave her in bed, she'd give him nothing out of it.

It was exactly what he'd asked for.

The drive to Kowhai the next day was predictably tense, even more so because of what had happened the previous night. Exhausted by his lovemaking, she'd fallen into a deep sleep. If Gabe hadn't given a short, choked cry and jerked upright sometime in the darkest hours, she might not have woken till morning.

Startled and half-asleep, she'd put her hand on his shoulder. "Gabe?"

"Go back to sleep." He'd gotten out of bed, uncaring of the moon's light on his nakedness.

"Did you have a nightmare?" Her voice had been

soft, her heart unshielded. She'd forgotten she wasn't supposed to care.

"I *said,* go back to sleep." Brutal in its coldness, the sharp command had thrown her tenderness back in her face. "Since you're up, it might be better if you went back to your own room."

Stung, she'd done just that, but finding herself unable to sleep, had spent the rest of the night working in her studio. Gabe hadn't slept either—she'd heard him leave the house not to return till after dawn.

Now here they sat, both of them punchy from lack of sleep and a relationship going steadily downhill.

She finally couldn't take the silence anymore. "How long will your meeting take?"

"Not long." He shifted gears as they neared a hill. "I forgot to give you your credit and debit cards so you'll have to use one of mine. Remind me to give it to you when we get to Kowhai."

She could hardly refuse his money when she'd spent the past year living on it, but it had never made her feel good about herself. Still didn't. "If Richard likes my work and is able to sell it, I'll have some income."

"That's not a problem, Jess. You're my wife." The words were almost absent-minded as he overtook a big truck.

Of course it was nothing to him—Gabe held all the cards in this marriage. She'd been in his debt from the instant he'd saved her family home.

He turned down the street leading into town. "I'll park at the post office."

"That sounds fine." Kowhai wasn't much but it was okay for a town in the middle of nowhere. There was a grocery store cum post office, a bank, the obligatory pub and even a small medical clinic along with some other shops. "Doesn't seem like it's changed much."

"Henry's handed over the running of the grocery store to Eddie."

"At last! How's he handling it?"

"You can ask him yourself." He nodded toward the store as they eased into one of the parking spaces out front.

Eddie was standing outside soaking up the sun and saw her the second she jumped out. Jogging over, he gave her a quick hug and a kiss on the cheek. "Jessie! Hey stranger. Hi, Mr. Dumont."

Jess blinked at the formal way he'd addressed Gabe. "Gabe's got to head off so can you help me get some packages to the post desk?"

Gabe interrupted before Eddie could reply. "I have time." Opening the door, he picked up the two biggest canvasses.

Nonplussed, Jess handed two more to Eddie and took the last one herself. They weren't that heavy, just awkward to carry, wrapped as they were for safe transport.

Eddie didn't speak again till Gabriel had left for his meeting. "You have to fill out one of these." He slid a courier slip toward her then lounged against the ledge that served as a table.

Jess began to complete the form. "Don't you have customers in the grocery section?"

"Sally can handle it—we're not too busy right now," he said, referring to his younger sister. "So, married to Gabriel Dumont, huh?"

"Mr. Dumont?" she teased.

He shrugged. "That's what I always called him when I used to work in the store after school. He's what, ten years older than you?"

"Nine," she corrected automatically, Eddie's tone beginning to irritate her.

"Yeah, well I was sure surprised to hear the news about the wedding."

Form filled in, she put down the pen. "Why?"

"Come on, Jess. When Damon left Kayla everyone thought it'd finally be him and you like it always should've been."

Of course Gabriel chose that moment to walk in. He passed her a credit card, no expression on his face. "You'll need this. Meet you back at the car in an hour."

"Okay."

He left without another word. Eddie winced when she turned back to him. "Sorry if I stuck my foot in it."

"Don't worry about it." If only she could follow her own advice. "But do me a favor and stop talking about me and Damon in the same breath, all right? I'm married and so is he."

"That's not what he said a few days ago at the pub. He didn't find out about your wedding until it was over, you know. He never figured Dumont would push you through it so fast. He said that if—"

"Don't." Jess raised a hand, palm out. "I don't want to hear it. How much for the courier?"

Taking the hint at last, Eddie processed her packages without further commentary. But when she went to pay, he let out a long whistle. "Platinum card, Jess? You sure have moved up in the world."

She chose to ignore the dig. People could believe what they liked. "Thanks." She took the receipt. "See you."

"Bye."

There was plenty of time left so she decided to say hello to some of the other people she knew in town.

However the first person she saw along the sidewalk was no one she wanted to meet. Unfortunately, she'd already been spotted.

"Jess!" Sylvie waved.

Knowing the gossip would spread like wildfire if she ignored the woman, Jess dug up her best fake smile. "Hello, Sylvie."

"What luck to see you here when I was thinking of you a second ago. I'm throwing myself a birthday bash, an intimate dinner party. I'd love for you and Gabe to come."

Jess couldn't think of anything she'd like less than to be stuck in a confined gathering with Sylvie. "I'll talk to—"

The blonde cut her off with a blinding smile. "Oh sorry, I should've said. I ran into Gabe at the bank and he said he'd be there."

Pre-warned by that smug smile, Jess maintained her composure. If Sylvie wanted to see her bleed, she'd have to find a sharper knife. "When's the party?"

"This Saturday. Around seven for cocktails at my place. See you there."

Jess made a noncommittal noise and they parted ways. Straightening the fingers she'd curled into fists inside her jacket pockets, she strode toward the bank. Gabe stepped out seconds after it came into view. Their eyes met and she found herself watching him walk to her, stunned anew by the impact of his presence. *Dear God.* If he could do this to her in public, then she was in desperate straits.

"Were you looking for me?"

Shaken, she barely noticed the hint of a smile on his face. "I met Sylvie on the way over." The memory was precisely what she needed to cut through the cloudy haze of desire.

"And?" He raised an eyebrow.

"And don't you think it would be nice if you spoke to me before accepting certain invitations?"

"If you have a problem with going, we can cancel."

"That's not the point. I know what you think of this marriage," she said, trying not to let emotion color her words, "but I deserve respect. You should've spoken to me."

"It's a party, Jess." He put his arm around her shoulders and began walking. "Nothing serious."

She went along rather than make a scene. "Maybe I don't want to go play nice with your ex-mistress."

With his body aligned to hers, there was no way she could miss his sudden tension. "If I'm not mistaken, that implies I kept her. Sylvie is more than capable of keeping herself."

Face burning at the subtle reminder that he *was* keeping Jess, she refused to look up and meet his mocking gaze. "You know what I mean. She's not my friend. I have no intention of going to that party."

"Fine. I'll go alone."

That answer only increased her fury. Taking her hands out of her pockets, she folded her arms across her chest. "No, you won't." Thankfully, they'd reached the car by then.

He stopped walking and released her. "Excuse me?" A very quiet, very lethal sound.

Difficult as it was to stand her ground, she wouldn't be able to face herself in the mirror if she didn't. "You don't want me to see Damon. Fine. But that works both ways. You don't get a free pass to socialize with your old lovers either."

"The difference, *Jessica* darling, is that I don't go

around avowing my undying love for Sylvie. And I sure as hell don't crawl all over her every time she so much as crooks a finger." He took out the car keys. "You can come to the dinner or not, but you haven't been paying attention if you think you have the ability to stop me from going."

Jess wanted to scream. Because he was right—in a battle of wills, she'd always lose. Gabe had been tempered in the most cruel of circumstances and it had hardened him to all that was soft and gentle. He'd never bend for a woman, most especially not a woman he'd bought and married on the understanding that she'd expect nothing from him.

Ever.

Several days passed in a procession of tense words and strained silences, with Jess keeping her distance while she figured out what to do. If she went to Sylvie's party, Gabe would win yet another skirmish in their ongoing war. But if she didn't, then that blond bitch would undoubtedly try something to ensnare Gabe. And Jess was discovering she had a rather wide streak of possessiveness where her husband was concerned. Something else she'd neither expected nor prepared for.

Of course, staying away from Gabe only worked during the day. During the night, she was his. In spite of everything, she'd come to crave the way he made her feel—so alive, so passionate, so intrinsically female. There was also another, less obvious temptation—she'd begun to believe that bed was the one place where Gabe might allow his ironclad control over his emotions to slip.

Sometimes, in the midst of the deepest intimacy, she thought she caught glimpses of the man behind the mask, fleeting moments of vulnerability and true feeling. If she could only push him further, make him remove that mask in other surroundings, she might yet discover the answers she so desperately needed…discover whether their marriage had a heart or was only a barren field. But Gabe never let her go that far, retreating behind his titanium-strong walls as soon as their bodies separated.

"Enough, Jess." She slashed paint onto a canvas and told herself to stop thinking about the things that took place in the lush intimacy of Gabriel's bed. Which left her mind free to stew over the party—now only two nights away. And about the fact that she hadn't heard from Richard Dusevic. A glob of paint flicked off her brush and onto the canvas.

"Damn it!" She decided to stop before she ruined the painting altogether.

A quick shower later, she grabbed the keys to the SUV and left Angel, not giving herself the opportunity to change her mind. She'd been a coward long enough.

It was time to go home.

To the main house on Randall Station, the place where she'd watched her father die a quiet death, safe in the knowledge that Jess would protect their land. Tears burned the backs of her eyes. Fighting them, she clamped her hands on the steering wheel and stared out at the passing scenery.

It was maybe sixty minutes later that the station-house first came into view, getting larger as she approached. And then there it was. Tempting as it was to turn the SUV around, she shut off the engine and stepped out.

She'd half expected to find it falling to pieces, but it

appeared to have been well maintained. Going up onto the verandah, she peered through the glass and gave a shocked gasp when she saw all their old furniture sitting inside, carefully covered with dust cloths.

Emotion a knot in her throat, she put her hand on the doorknob. It was locked, of course. She'd never returned after being evicted by the bank, but now she wondered if anyone had bothered to change the locks.

Running back down the steps, she reached under the last one and scrabbled around until she located a small rock. "Gotcha!" The key was rusty but otherwise fine. Dusting off her knees, she went to try the lock. If it *had* been changed, she'd have to ask Gabe for the new key and, in her current mood, she didn't want to ask him for anything.

She slid the slender piece of metal into the lock and turned. "Please. Please let me in."

Eight

The door opened in smooth welcome. Kicking off her shoes out of habit, she walked through the hallway and into the living room. It hurt. So many memories, so many good times. But walking into the kitchen was the worst. This was the heart of the house, where she and her father had sat many a night drinking coffee and talking over everything.

Everything but the finances it turned out.

Sean Randall had considered it a man's duty to take care of his family, to keep a roof over their heads. So he'd borne the strain alone and she'd been too wrapped up in the cotton-wool of his love to understand the threat of foreclosure.

But then he'd died, leaving her with the burden of a promise she'd sacrificed everything to keep. "How could you do that to me, Dad?" Sobs breaking her voice, she crumpled to the floor. Guilt had kept her from acknowledging the anger she'd carried around since his death, but being in this house destroyed her ability to pretend.

When the tears finally stopped, she felt wrung dry. There was no water in the taps so she walked out to the SUV, found one of the bottles of water always banging around in the back, and used it to wash her face. Afterward, she had no will to return to the house. It belonged to the ghosts now.

Instead, she went down on her knees in front of the verandah and began to pull weeds. While the building had been maintained, Beth Randall's garden had been left to run wild, a tangle of climbers and weeds even in the still-icy breath of winter's approaching end.

"Look after my garden won't you, Jessie my love?"

"Yes, Mom," she'd said, holding on to her mother as she lay dying in the hospital bed.

A promise to her mother. And one to her father. Between them, they held her trapped. A trap of emotion, of love, of memory.

Where the hell was Jess? Gabe stared out at the cloud-heavy evening sky and swore he'd wring her fool neck when he found her. "Are you sure she didn't say where she was going?"

Mrs. C. shook her head. "She wasn't here when I came back from Kowhai. I figured she'd gone visiting."

"I'm heading out to have a look. If she comes back, tell her to stay put."

"Do you want me to ring around?"

"I'll give you a call if I don't find her." He held up his cell phone and made a mental note to buy one for Jess as well. "Why don't you go home?"

"Are you sure?"

"You can keep an eye out for her from the cottage—
the driveway's in your line of sight." He got into the Jeep
after receiving a nod of understanding. As he backed up
and turned in the drive, he considered the places where
his wife might have gone without leaving word, especially when she was pissed with him.

His jaw tightened. No, surely even Jess wouldn't be
idiotic enough to wave the red flag of Damon in front
of him. Deciding to give her the benefit of the doubt, he
headed toward the one place that he knew held a grip
over her stronger than anything or anyone else.

Bumpy country roads made the drive slow going and
when full dark caught up with him near the old
boundary line, he had to further lower his speed. By the
time he got to what had once been the Randall station
house, he was cursing himself for not having gone with
his first instinct and hunting down that pretty-boy Jess
was in love with.

All that changed a few meters later when his headlights bounced off the side of the SUV. There was no
one inside. Worry jackknifed in his gut. If she'd injured
herself, she could have been lying out here for hours.
Alert for any sign of her, he brought the Jeep around,
intending to park it parallel to the other vehicle.

The headlights swept across a small figure seated on
the verandah steps, hand raised to block the brightness.
His concern flashfired into the most dangerous kind of
anger in a single hard instant. Turning off the lights and
engine, he got out.

"Gabe?" She gave him a puzzled look. "What are you
doing here?"

"Looking for you, that's what." He pulled her to her

feet. "What the hell kind of childish stunt do you think you're pulling?"

"Stunt?" Something in Jess broke at that moment. She slammed her fists into his shoulders. "I came to visit the only place that's ever been home to me! To be close to the only people who ever loved me! Can't you even allow me that?"

"Stop it." He pulled her into a tight embrace to restrain her pummeling hands. "Be still, Jessie."

She struggled to escape but he was holding her so tightly, she could hardly move. "Damn you, you've never loved anyone in your life! How would you know what it feels like to lose everything?" His body went as still as ice, but blinded by her own anguish, she paid no attention. "You don't even put flowers on their graves!"

"Shut up. Shut the hell up before you say anything else." Quiet, frighteningly calm, his tone cut through her pained fury to chill her on the inside.

"Why?" she challenged, refusing to be bullied. "Don't you like hearing the truth?"

He released her so suddenly she almost her balance. "What do you know about the truth?" The words were razor-sharp, edged by blades of contained rage.

"I know your father changed the name of Dumont Station to Angel Station because your mother loved angels and he loved her." Everyone in Kowhai knew that story.

He swore, harsh and bullet-fast. "Yeah, the great Dumont romance."

His flippant response bruised her and she didn't quite understand why. "Just because you're made of stone doesn't mean you have the right to mock their love!"

"I have every right!" His voice rose for the first time

and he shoved up a shirt-sleeve to bare the faded burn scars on his arm. "I *earned* that right."

Shocked out of her self-absorption by the sheer depth of his anger, she frowned. "What are you talking about?" Her eyes fell to his scars. "What do your burns have to do with your parents?"

"Everything." A grim statement.

"But, the fire was an accident."

His entire demeanor changed in a millisecond. It was like watching a wall descend over his face. Pushing down the sleeve, he jerked his head toward the cars. "Get in. We have to drive back before the rain hits."

She gripped his arm. "Gabe? What did you mean?" He'd come close to telling her something important.

His answer was to remove her hand and say, "I'll go in front. Follow as close as you can—the tracks can be difficult at night." None of his earlier fury was now evident but she'd felt the tension thrumming beneath the surface of his skin.

"You can't do this," she protested. "I'm your wife. I have a right to know about your past."

"Why do you keep making me remind you of the terms of our marriage?" he asked almost conversationally, eyes black in the darkness. "The only thing you have a right to know is that I can provide a good home for you and the child you agreed to bear me. If you have any doubts about that, I'll show you the accounts tomorrow."

She knew he was being purposefully cruel in order to block her questions but that didn't make it hurt any less. What she didn't stop to consider was why it hurt. "You're calling me a gold-digger?"

"No, Jess. I always thought it a fair deal. How else

could I have found a woman willing to agree to never make any waves in my life?" He opened the door of the Jeep. "So concentrate on doing a better job of keeping up your end of the bargain. I don't want anything else from you."

That night, Jess lay awake in her bed, waiting for Gabe to come for her as he always did. But the hours passed and the door between their rooms remained shut. An odd feeling clawed through her veins. Surely she wasn't disappointed? No, of course not. It was simply that she'd wanted a chance to push Gabriel into talking about what he'd alluded to earlier.

"Stop lying to yourself," she whispered out loud. "Talking is hardly what you do best in bed." And though it was tempting to place the responsibility for the heavily sexual nature of their marriage on Gabe, she knew she was as much to blame. If she hadn't been so eager a lover, would he have become as demanding?

Kicking off the blankets in a burst of frustration, she folded her arms behind her head. It was obvious that Gabe was very angry over what she'd said tonight. But his wrath had never before stopped him from claiming her. It would seem she'd touched a raw nerve. What she couldn't understand was how.

There was no mystery around the fire—it had been ruled an accident. Then she remembered that it had been the mention of his parents' love that had first set him off. She'd grown up hearing stories of how Stephen Dumont had wed Mary Hannah the day of her high school graduation. Though he'd been fifteen years her senior, they'd become inseparable from day one, and had had four children in quick succession.

Why would the reminder of such a bright love enrage Gabe?

"Stop thinking and start doing, Jess." Getting up, she pulled on a robe. Gabe might think he'd silenced her with his cruel reference to the terms of their marriage, but she wasn't so easily distracted. Maybe, she thought, remembering his nightmare, she'd come too close to whatever it was that haunted him…hurt him. It was time to find out for certain.

However the master bedroom proved to be empty. Guessing that Gabe hadn't yet come up from his study, she padded downstairs and along the corridor. The light spilling out from the half-open door at the end confirmed her guess.

She placed her fingers on the wood, ready to push it open. Then Gabriel spoke and what he said made her turn to stone.

"She knows nothing about it and it's going to stay that way." A short silence. "How I handle my wife is my concern." Another short pause. "No, Sylvie won't say anything. I've already spoken to her."

Jess stuffed a fist into her mouth to stifle her cry. Gabe had told his secrets to his one-time lover, but he wouldn't even consider telling his wife?

"There won't be a problem. Jess won't rock the boat."

She began to back away from the door, trying to not make a sound. *God, she was stupid.* If Gabriel's earlier statements hadn't made it perfectly clear, it was obvious from the way he'd just spoken that he really did consider her nothing more than a convenience. A wife who'd give him a child and otherwise stay out of his life. A wife who'd never *rock the boat*. And here she'd come down with some half-baked notion of helping him face his demons.

"So concentrate on doing a better job of keeping up your end of the bargain. I don't want anything else from you."

Why had she rationalized away that statement? The question tormented Jess as she made her way to her studio. Once inside, she turned on the light and shut the door but refused to give in to the urge to cry, though it thrust a knife through her to think of Gabe sharing his secrets with Sylvie. That was a reaction she didn't want to examine too closely.

Because it could not be allowed to continue. At least tonight's humiliation had finally screwed her head on straight, crushing the fragile dreams she'd unconsciously begun to build despite everything she'd told herself to the contrary. The only way she was going to survive this marriage was to do as Gabe had done and bury her emotions so deep, nothing and no one could ever reach her.

Picking up a brush almost automatically, she began to put the final touches on Damon's portrait. Minutes, maybe longer passed. She was composed enough to not betray anything when the door snicked open and Gabe walked in.

"I thought you were asleep."

She made no effort to hide the portrait as he came around to stand beside her. He stared at it without speaking as she made the last stroke and stepped back. "Finished."

"Yes," Gabe agreed, a tightness to his tone she had no trouble reading. "That part of your life is over."

Putting away the palette and brush, she checked her hands and found not a speck of paint on them. "As your relationship with Sylvie is over?" She regretted the words the second they were out—obviously, she wasn't as good as Gabriel at shutting off her emotions. "Forget it."

"I'm not sleeping with anyone but you," was his blunt rejoinder.

"I said forget it." Having tidied up, she was ready to leave but Gabe blocked her way.

Leaning in, he curled a strand of her hair around his fingers, then released it. "I don't think I want to. Are you jealous, Jess?" He almost sounded amused but there was an intensity to his eyes that held not laughter but a wealth of unrelenting hunger.

That quickly, the atmosphere shifted from edgy to lushly sensual. When he bent his head to hers, she stood her ground with a sense of fatalism. He'd hurt her with the way he'd dismissed her so easily, hurt her so much. But at this moment, she couldn't move away and part of her despised herself for it. The rest of her ached for his touch.

If the harsh jangle of the phone hadn't torn the passionate web to pieces, she might yet have surrendered the remaining tatters of her pride.

Swearing under his breath, Gabe picked up the portable handset she'd appropriated for this room and barked out a rough, "Hello." His face froze over almost instantly. "It's one in the morning."

Jess didn't know how she knew it was Damon calling, but when she held out her hand, Gabriel slammed the receiver into her palm. "Get rid of him," was his terse instruction.

Thankful he'd at least passed her the phone, she didn't get in much more than a word before Damon began to speak. Gabe gave her a disgusted look when she didn't immediately hang up, and started to leave. She grabbed the front of his shirt. "Wait."

Covering the mouthpiece, she looked into her husband's furious eyes. "Something's wrong with Kayla. They're at the clinic with Dr. Mackey and Damon's losing it. He thinks they might not be able to save the baby."

If he'd shaken off her hand, she wouldn't have been surprised. But what he did was take the phone and speak directly to Damon. "Jess is going to get changed. We'll be there soon as we can."

Nine

By the time they got to Kowhai, the rescue chopper was on its way. But Dr. Mackey—the one who met them at the clinic door—was clearly still very worried.

"Can you tell us what's happening?" Jess asked. "Damon said something about the baby…."

"Kayla's looking like she might go into premature labor. I've put her on meds to delay it but…" He shook his head. "That's not actually the worst of it—her blood pressure's far too high for safety."

Jess didn't need to be told that the clinic had neither the equipment nor the resources to deal with either half of the situation. "What do you want us to do?"

"Get Damon out of here. He's frantic and that's not helping. I'm going to go back in to check on her."

Damon walked out of the only patient room at that very moment. "Jess, I don't know what to do."

Hugging him close, she glanced over at Gabe. Her husband nodded.

"Come on," he said to the younger man. "Why don't you help me put out landing beacons in the parking lot?"

Looking glad to have something to do, Damon followed him out. Jess waited until Dr. Mackey had emerged from Kayla's room to ask if she could go sit with her.

"I think that would be good, Jess." Dr. Mackey rubbed at his eyes. "I'm going to call the hospital and make sure they're ready."

Walking into the room, Jess took a seat beside Kayla's bed, not sure what her welcome would be. "Hey."

The other woman's pale face broke out into a genuinely relieved smile. "Oh, Jess. I'm so glad you're here." When she held out a hand, Jess took it, wanting to help her in any way she could. The irony of being a comfort to the very woman who'd been the cause of what Jess had always considered her greatest heartbreak, wasn't lost on her. But at that moment, Kayla was in pain and Jess could do nothing but feel for her.

Twenty more nerve-wracking minutes later, the chopper arrived. "Gabe, will you tidy up the lights?" Dr. Mackey asked as he jumped in with his patient and Damon.

Gabe nodded. "Don't worry about it."

They stood aside as the chopper took off in a rush of wind, then set about clearing the mobile landing lights. The work went fast and they were on their way home not much later. When Gabe tugged her into his room after an exhausting ride back, she didn't argue.

They fell asleep intertwined and Jess had no thoughts of getting up any time soon. However Gabe stirred after

what had to have been only a couple of hours at most.
Jess knew stations didn't run themselves, but even in the
short time that she'd been his wife, she'd noticed he had
a real problem delegating authority.

"Let Jim handle things," she said, voice scratchy with
sleep. "Get a few more hours rest." Picking up the
phone, she passed it to him.

He looked down at her with an inscrutable expression. But he made the call and settled in beside her
again, tugging her body flush against his. Jess had a
moment to be amazed at the wonder of Gabe listening
to her before tiredness washed over in her in an inex-
orable wave.

"Damon rang," Jess told Gabe over dinner that night.
"Kayla's stable. They've also got the labor stopped for
now, but the doctors are keeping her under observation.
They think she might give birth despite the drugs."

"Do you want to go to the hospital?"

Their eyes met across the table, his revealing nothing
no matter how hard she tried to read them. "There's no
need. Damon's with her and he seems to be calm now."

"I wasn't thinking about Kayla."

The steel of the fork cut into her flesh, she was
squeezing it so hard. "I was." So, the fragile truce
formed between them in the early hours when they'd
helped Kayla and Damon was over. It was just as well.
She'd been in danger of forgetting the humiliating conversation she'd overheard last night—a conversation
which had proven beyond a shadow of a doubt that she
meant less than nothing to Gabe.

They finished the meal in silence and Jess went up
to her bedroom. However sleep was the last thing on her

mind—the situation with Kayla had set off a mental
warning bell earlier today. She'd only had to glance at
her diary to confirm the disquieting realization. Thankfully, she'd had the foresight to buy a testing kit in L.A.,
well aware that if she did the same in Kowhai, it'd be
all over town in about three seconds flat.

Not wanting to chance an interruption, she'd forced
herself to wait till after dinner and Gabe's retreat to his
study. Now she had a bare minute's wait left, a minute that
could change her life forever. Emotions crashed through
her like thunder. Fear. Anticipation. Joy. Sheer terror.

She'd gone into this marriage blithely assuming she
could give Gabriel an heir. What she'd never once
factored into her decision was how she'd feel at bringing
a child into the world with a man who might never love
that child. How could he? Her husband seemed inca-
pable of any tenderness.

The timer on her watch went off.

Looking down at the indicator, she steeled herself for
either result. *"Oh."*

Somehow, she was on the bathroom floor, her entire
body a mass of tremors. Her first instinct was to tell
Gabriel but something stopped her. She needed time to
get used to the idea herself, time to build shields around
the huge vulnerability that had just opened up in her
heart and soul.

She was going to have a baby.

Gabriel's baby.

And the second he found out, she'd lose any hope she
had of making him see her as something other than a
vehicle to give him his heir. Jess couldn't let that
happen, though she also couldn't articulate why. It
simply seemed integral that there be an indefinable *more*

between them. But if Gabe learned about the baby, he'd see no reason to change—not when he could have everything he wanted on his terms.

No, she couldn't tell him. Not yet.

Despite her utter certainty that she'd made the right decision, she barely slept that night and spent most of the next day trying to come to terms with her pregnancy. Her nerves were frayed to a breaking point by the time she slipped into a simple black dress that evening. Sleeveless and with a scooped neckline that barely skimmed her cleavage, it kissed the top edge of her knees and followed the lines of her body.

It was the sexiest dress she owned. Which wasn't saying much—Sylvie was certain to be draped in something stunning.

Jess's gaze drifted to the closet…to the wine-red sheath she'd bought in a mad moment and never worn. And if she didn't get around to wearing it soon, it wasn't going to fit.

"Stop thinking about it. You'll need all your wits tonight." Giving a decisive nod, she put her foot on the bed and picked up a fine black stocking topped with lace.

She had the second one halfway up her leg when Gabriel pushed through the door. She went motionless as his eyes trailed up her leg and over the bare skin of her thigh. And then he began to walk toward her. Dressed in a pair of black pants and a deep green shirt that seemed oddly familiar, he was enough to stop any woman in her tracks…even one as conflicted as Jess.

Coming to a standstill beside her, he put a hand on her raised knee. A prisoner to her own inexplicable need, she watched as he bent to place a single kiss on her upper thigh. Shockwaves of sensation rocked through her. And she knew that for all its gentleness, it was a brand, a silent statement that she belonged to him.

When he straightened to his full height, the raw desire in his eyes threatened to burn. "Finish it."

She should have protested his order but her mind was out of her control, hijacked by the potent masculinity of this man she lacked the power to resist. His finger traced the lace edge as she completed the task, but he made no effort to stop her from putting her foot on the floor. Yet even with both feet on the ground, she couldn't quite find her sense of balance.

"I need to put on my shoes." The words came out on a breathy whisper that sounded like an invitation.

Placing his hands on her shoulders, Gabe turned her so she faced away from him. She was about to ask him what he wanted when he stroked his hands down her side, fingers tracing over the curves of her breasts.

She screamed at herself to resist but her body was already caught in the web Gabe alone could weave. Reaching her hips, he tugged up her dress, bunching it in his hands until the hemline hovered at the top edge of her stockings. Shocked at the clawing power of the need inside of her, she tried to back away from herself but ended up with her body flush against his.

His lips met the curve of her neck even as the hardness of his arousal thrust against her, further electrifying senses saturated almost past bearing. "Gabe." It was a plea.

He ran his lips along the shell of one ear. "Hold your dress for me."

Once again, she knew she shouldn't obey, shouldn't give in to him. He'd destroy her defenses when she needed them so desperately tonight. But her hands were moving before the thought ended, her body a stranger to her will. Letting her take over the task, he ran his hands up along her sides and then, to her surprise, pulled back.

Feeling oddly ambivalent about the reprieve, she motioned to drop the hem. He pressed against her once more. "Hold it." A soft command coated with the authority of a man used to giving them.

She scowled. "Why?"

"Because I'm otherwise occupied." He nudged her gently forward until she stood in front of the mirror.

"What—?"

"This." He strung something cool and beautiful around her neck.

"Gabe!" The glitter of the teardrop emerald flickered in the mirror, its brightness cradled by the soft darkness of the valley between her breasts.

Closing the clasp, Gabe stroked his fingers along the gold of the necklace to pick up the emerald. His knuckles brushed the upper curve of her breast, causing her to hold her breath until he replaced the pendant in the valley for which it seemed tailor-made.

"Beautiful." One of his hands came to rest on her hip.

"I can't—" she began, stunned at the expensive gift.

"No arguments." Moving around her, he leaned his body against the vanity and pulled her into the vee of his thighs.

She finally dropped the hem. "Why? We're fighting." Her hand drifted to the cool beauty of the emerald.

In response, he ran his own hands up under her dress, shocking a short, ultimately feminine sound out of her. Releasing the emerald, she braced herself against his shoulders.

"You're my wife," he said, as if that was reason enough.

"But you've—"

He kissed the words from her lips, his hands sliding around the back of her thighs to cup her bottom. His hold was incredibly intimate and when he pulled her closer, she went, wrapping her arms around his neck.

His fingers traced the edge of her panties. "What color?" he asked against her mouth.

"Black." Her heart slammed into her ribs with punishing force. There was something very possessive in Gabriel's eyes tonight, something untamed and wild and all the more exhilarating for it. Her next words came from a part of her that she hadn't known existed until this moment. "And so is the bra. A matching set."

He smiled and it was so slow and satisfied, her stomach tumbled. "Jessica darling, are you trying to make us late to the party? Your way of winning our little stand-off?"

In truth, she'd forgotten about it. "You're the one who interrupted me." She was blindingly conscious of one of his hands moving to the front of her body.

Ten

"So I did," he murmured, reclaiming her lips even as his hand pushed aside the gusset of her panties to thrust two fingers deep into a body more than primed by the slow seduction. Pleasure erupted inside her almost instantaneously. Pulling away from the ravaging fury of his mouth, she threw back her head and rode his fingers, feeling herself clench and unclench with vicious strength. She was on the verge of an explosive climax when he withdrew them.

Dazed, she swayed on her feet as he switched position to stand behind her. Instinct made her brace her hands on the vanity, her hair a tumbling mess around her face. When she raised her hand to push it back, she caught sight of the primal intensity driving Gabe—her husband was *not* in control tonight. That was all the warning she got before he shoved up her dress and slid inside her.

Crying out, she tried to move with him, but his rhythm was too fast for her to follow. "Please, please, please." The whimpers were so needy she couldn't believe they were her own.

Gabe's arm came around her waist and his teeth scraped lightly over the sensitive skin of her neck. "Now, Jess. Now!"

She fractured under the command, everything female in her glorying in the wildness of that harsh masculine voice. At the last second, their eyes met in the mirror and Jess knew they'd crossed a line. The question was, what lay on the other side?

They were forty minutes late to the party. Jess's dress had been wrinkled beyond repair, so after a quick shower shared with a surprisingly playful Gabe, she'd put on a fitting pencil skirt and thin V-neck cardigan, both in black. The pendant glowed against her flushed skin. Gabe had insisted she put her stockings back on and she'd acquiesced—she liked the idea of him thinking her sexy, especially since Sylvie was going to be around.

Gabe's shirt, on the other hand, had emerged magically unscathed and he'd pulled it back on. It was only as they were walking through Sylvie's door that Jess realized the color almost perfectly matched his eyes. She scowled. Gabe might be wealthy and powerful, but he was also a man's man—fashion was not in his repertoire. The fact that he'd chosen something with that much care for Sylvie's party, stuck in her craw, dispelling what remained of the sensual afterglow.

The birthday girl beamed at Gabe, giving him a kiss on the cheek in return for his gift of a bottle of premier wine. "That green does wonderful things for your eyes, darling."

Jess wondered if it would be catty to ask why she didn't deserve a welcome kiss, too. Amused by the thought, she leaned into Gabe's hold. Sylvie's eyes went straight to the emerald. She covered it well but Jess glimpsed a definite spark of anger. And no matter how petty it was, that reaction made her very happy.

"I can't take any of the credit. Jess is the one responsible."

Jess was so startled by Gabe's comment she couldn't say a word.

"I didn't know you had such a good eye." Sylvie gave her a bright smile that could have cut glass. "You're always so…simply dressed."

"I prefer to leave things to the imagination." Jess smiled and pointedly avoided glancing at the plunging neckline of her rival's very short black dress. The irritating thing was that Sylvie looked sexy when anyone else wearing that outfit would have crossed the line into trashy.

Thankfully, another late arrival entered behind them and they were able to move on.

"What did you mean about me being responsible?" she asked the second they were out of earshot.

He raised an eyebrow. "Last year, my birthday."

"Oh." Now she remembered sending him that spontaneous gift. "I wasn't sure I got the size right." Or that he'd even like it.

He ran his knuckles down her cheek. "Obviously you were keeping an eye on my body long before you left."

Blushing, she couldn't help but recall their wild encounter in front of her mirror. Gabe smiled and reached over to pick up two flutes of wine from the tray of a passing waiter.

Jess found her wits quickly. "Actually, can I have juice?"

He switched her drink and handed it over. "I thought you liked white wine."

"I don't feel like it tonight," she lied, wondering how long it would take him to figure out why she didn't want to drink. Gabe had a mind more efficient than many a computer but maybe this one time he'd be blind for a little while longer.

At that moment, a landowner Jess knew only vaguely walked over. "Gabriel, I've been wanting to talk to you."

Smiling at the man's wife, Jess made small talk for a few minutes before another couple joined them and picked up the conversational ball. It left her free to observe and the foremost thing she noticed was that she was standing in the midst of the most powerful people in the room.

The second was that even the older ones looked to Gabe for advice, their respect for him far deeper than she'd ever realized. For the first time, she had a misgiving about their marriage unconnected to Gabe's inability to offer the slightest crumb of tenderness.

Although she'd grown up on a station, it had been a very small one and her father had never taught her the business side of things. Neither was she an accomplished hostess or conversationalist, when it was patent that Gabe needed all those things in his wife. She wouldn't go so far as to call herself a country bumpkin, but she *was* moving in social circles way beyond her own.

"Everything all right here?" Sylvie slid into the group on Gabe's other side.

"It's a fabulous party," one of the older women exclaimed. "The perfect mix of people."

"I wanted to keep things intimate, limit it to my close friends."

Jess knew Sylvie wasn't grandstanding. Part of a respected and wealthy family, she'd grown up circulating amongst these people. Jess was the odd woman out.

"I think dinner's ready to be served," Sylvie announced. "Why don't we head into the dining room? I've put place cards at the table—thought it'd be fun for us to mingle."

Jess had an odd feeling she knew exactly where the other woman would be sitting and with whom. She wasn't far off the mark. Though Sylvie hadn't placed herself at the head of the table but in the middle, she'd put Gabriel to her right and another man to her left.

Jess faced the birthday girl, having been sandwiched between a woman known nationwide for her society parties, and a fashionably dressed male who she thought was supposed to be Sylvie's official date.

Gabe stood up, wineglass in hand. Everyone went silent. "Since Sylvie's parents are out of the country, she's asked me to do the toast." He looked down at the other woman. "I think you'd all agree that Sylvie's achieved some amazing things with her career at a very young age."

Jess gripped her hands together under the table, telling herself that Gabe's comments were no reflection on her.

"She has every reason to be happy with where she is today and to celebrate this birthday with pride. I invite you all to join me in congratulating her on everything she's accomplished so far and will continue to accomplish. Happy birthday Sylvie."

Cheers sounded around the table and a beaming Sylvie put her hand on Gabe's arm as he sat back down. Jess made herself look away by sheer effort of will. She refused to give Sylvie the satisfaction of appearing a needy, jealous wife. At that second, her eyes clashed into those of the man beside her.

He smiled. "I'm Jason."

"Jess." She tried to relax. "So, Jason, what do you do?"

"I'm a lawyer, I'm afraid. Oh, excuse me." He turned away to answer a question from the woman on his other side.

"Jessica, my dear, I've been waiting to speak to you."

Surprised, Jess looked to her left. "Mrs. Kilpatrick?" What could they possibly have to speak about?

"Why didn't you tell me you were such an artist?"

Caught completely by surprise, Jess lowered the juice glass she'd just picked up. "But how did you know?"

"Would you believe I've been friends with Richard Dusevic for years? Last week we were both in Australia for an important show. The whole time, he was champing at the bit to get back because his assistant had rung to say that the package from J.B. Randall had arrived." Mrs. Kilpatrick's smile lit up her whole face. "After all that, I had to see the paintings for myself, so I stopped by his gallery before flying down last night."

Jess looked up at the sound of Sylvie's laughter and found Gabe smiling at the blonde in a way he never did for his wife. Stomach in knots, she forced her attention back to Mrs. Kilpatrick.

"You could've knocked me over with a feather when I found out J.B. Randall was none other than our very own Jessie!"

"So, Richard liked my work?" Jess asked, hand threatening to crush the glass as Sylvie laughed for the second time.

"Oh, listen to me blather on. I made him promise that

I'd be the one to tell you, being that I've known you since you were a child. He wants to put on a solo show for you!"

Jess was stunned—a solo show for an unknown artist was almost unheard of. But even the depth of her excitement at the astonishing opportunity couldn't quell the anger she felt at seeing Sylvie continue to flirt outrageously with Gabriel. He didn't seem to be encouraging her but neither was he doing anything to halt her.

"Will you do me a favor?" Jason asked a few minutes later after Mrs. Kilpatrick's attention had been claimed by someone else.

"What?" She wrenched her eyes from the couple across the table. "Oh, sure. What is it?"

The handsome man leaned close. "Flirt with me."

"Excuse me?"

"Look," he said, putting an arm along the back of her chair, "this might be Sylvie's party, but she invited me here as her date."

"So?"

"So the fact that she's apparently planning to ignore me the whole night is not sitting well." He raised an eyebrow. "And if I'm not mistaken, it's your husband she's trying to reel in."

Jess narrowed her eyes. "Gabriel isn't that easily led."

"But don't you want to make him a little uncomfortable? Stupidly childish of us, I admit, but I don't see him stopping her."

"He can hardly move away," Jess argued, though she'd had the exact same thought mere seconds ago. Something in her was very, very angry at Gabriel right now. Given what she'd overheard two nights ago, it was blatantly clear that he and Sylvie had had a far deeper relationship than she'd ever before realized. He might have married Jess, but it was Sylvie to whom he'd told his secrets. And that was a betrayal Jess couldn't forgive.

Jason leaned closer. "Would it help to know that your husband has suddenly developed an interest in our side of the table?"

It took a huge effort for her to not look in Gabe's direction. "I suppose you think that's your doing?"

"Of course it is. I'm rich, gorgeous and successful, not to mention charming."

"You're a menace, too." She laughed despite herself.

Something in Jason's face underwent a subtle change. "You know, I think I want to flirt with you for real."

"Contain yourself." Jess knew she was treading dangerous waters but she didn't give a damn. However it had nothing to do with Jason. He was nice enough and undeniably charming, but the man at the center of her thoughts sat on the other side of the table.

Her mind screeched to a halt. Since when had Gabriel become the man she thought about most often? It had always been Damon who occupied that special place in her heart and soul. But now Gabriel was there and that terrified her.

"Do you ever travel up to Auckland?" Jason asked, retrieving a business card from his pocket.

She smiled at the thought of the proposed show. "I will be soon."

"Visit me." He passed her his card.

Jess put it carefully beside her plate. "I'm married."

"Doesn't stop some."

"It stops me." She held his gaze.

He gave a rueful shrug. "Keep the card anyway. You might need a lawyer someday and I'm damn good." Removing his arm from her chair, he reached for his wineglass and clicked it against the glass she'd just picked up.

Jess managed to keep her head down until after she'd taken a sip of juice and spooned up some pudding. Her pragmatic nature said that Gabriel had likely not even noticed Jason's little charade, and even if he had, he'd hardly have taken it seriously. Still, something in her hoped otherwise.

Taking a quiet breath, she looked up…into the pure green focus of his eyes. All the air rushed out of her lungs and her hand rose to curl around the emerald. It was impossible not to relive the ecstasy of what had taken place between them after he'd put it on her, but she dropped her hand soon as she saw that same knowledge in the sardonic curve of his mouth.

However the damage had already been done. With a single look, Gabriel had let her know that he'd seen through her ridiculous attempt at provoking jealousy…and that it had meant nothing to him. Because in the end, she was his.

Bought and paid for.

A stab of unexpected pain bloomed in her heart. When had the truth gained the power to wound her so? She'd known the deal was a cold-hearted one when she'd made it. But suddenly it mattered that she'd sold herself in marriage to a man who'd never see her as a husband should see his wife.

She cursed herself for being a hypocrite even as that thought whispered through her mind. She didn't love Gabe, had always loved Damon. She had no right to complain if her husband, too, had given away his love long before she'd come into his life.

But it mattered. All at once, everything mattered.

* * *

Jess tossed her purse onto the vanity and kicked off her shoes before sitting down on the bed to remove her stockings.

Gabe walked in a second later. "There was a message from Richard Dusevic on the answering machine. He's going to call again tomorrow."

"Mrs. Kilpatrick already told me what it's about." She related the details without any of the excitement she'd always thought she'd feel at this moment.

"Congratulations. Do you have enough pieces for a show?" He crossed the carpet to stand in front of her seated form.

She felt the hairs on the back of her neck rise in primitive warning. "Some of the pieces you stored for me—from before L.A., are good enough, I think. And, I had a lot of time over the past year."

"You're a determined woman. I'm sure the show will be a success. But Jess," he used a finger to tip up her chin, "that game you were playing during dinner? Don't ever try it again."

Shocked at the quiet fury beneath the calm words, she stared at him. "Why not?" Self-preservation went out the window—she'd rather have Gabe's passion, even if it was in the form of anger, than a safe life. It would have been a startling realization had she been able to think logically. "Should I have sat there like a dumb rock while you looked down Sylvie's cleavage?"

He caught her chin between his thumb and forefinger. "No, my *darling* wife, that you can't accuse me of. If I want to see a woman's body, I do it in private. You, however, were putting on quite a show for your friend."

"Oh, please," she muttered. "I'm wearing a cardigan! How much more conservative could I get?"

"Right now, I can see straight down to the tops of your breasts and the edges of your bra." His tone was on the lethal side of dangerous.

Blushing, she resisted the urge to cross her arms over her chest. "You have a different vantage point. And that's not what I was getting at."

"Which was?"

She gripped the edge of the bed. "As you've pointed out on many occasions, you married me because I'd be a nice, easy, *well-behaved* wife who'd do what you wanted. Fine. I'll be that wife," she promised rashly. "But get one thing straight—I'm not some doormat you can tread on whenever you like, with whomever you please."

He released her chin and pulled her to her feet by her upper arms. "Be very careful what you accuse me of, Jess."

The sane woman in her said she should stop, that she was pushing him too far, but she was beyond rational thought. "Tell me, Gabe, is that why you wanted a compliant wife too much in your debt to dare make waves? So you'd be able to have your cake and eat it, too?"

Eleven

White lines bracketed his mouth. "I'm not the one who parades around wearing my love for another man like some kind of damn holy grail."

Her head snapped back from the chilling impact of his words.

Tightening his hold on her arms, he almost lifted her off the floor. "Don't think you're going to free yourself to chase after him by pinning false accusations of infidelity on me!"

"Do you really think I'd do something like that?" she whispered, bruised to the core. "His wife's in the hospital and they're about to have a baby."

"Cut the act, Jess. You were very good to Kayla but how much of that was because of guilt, huh?" Setting her free in a sudden movement, he thrust a hand through his hair. "If Damon walked into this room right this second and asked you to marry him, you'd accept in a shot, pregnant wife or not!"

Blood freezing in her veins, she dropped down to her previous position on the bed. "Get out." It was a quiet sound. "Leave me alone."

"That's your response to the truth, turn tail and hide?"

She raised her face, desperate to conceal the tears choking up her throat. "You just gave me a very good indication of what kind of a person you think I am— the kind who'd not only break her own marriage vows, but also ruin the life of a woman and an unborn child. Why would you want to be in a room with me anyway?"

Gabriel was asking himself the same question. Every time Jess got near Damon, she lit up like a damn light bulb. There was no doubt in his mind that if the chance presented itself, she'd always choose the other man. Gabe should have walked away the second he realized that. Instead, he'd married her.

And now he found himself no longer happy about her devotion to Damon, regardless of the fact that it was keeping her from asking things from him he had no desire to give. Worse, he couldn't seem to stay away from her. It was purely the sex, he told himself. Jess was a lover unlike any he'd ever had.

"I married you for things other than conversation," he said, furious with her both for her love for Damon and the way she'd flirted with that lawyer. "Having sex with you doesn't have to involve liking you."

Jess went very quiet for an instant. Then she stood and began undoing her cardigan. "Fine. Let's do it and get it over with so I can go to sleep."

"You think you can keep up that expressionless face after I touch you?" he taunted, pushed to the brink. Bed was the one place where she was utterly *his*. "The second I take you into my arms—"

"I might be in your arms," she interrupted, streaks of red high on her cheekbones, "but it's not you I'm thinking about."

Gabe felt every muscle in his body lock. Not trusting himself in the same room as her, he walked out and slammed the door behind him. Damn her. And damn him for being fool enough to think he could escape the curse of the past. He was, after all, his father's son.

Jess collapsed onto the bed and, muffling her sobs with her fist, tried not to think of anything. But her mind wouldn't stop. She was pregnant by a man who saw her as the worst kind of lying, cheating fraud.

And there was no way out. If she left him he'd sell her family home to the developers without the least hesitation. Gabriel Dumont hadn't reached his position in life by being thwarted. He'd made her his wife and he'd keep her his wife.

But something had changed inside of her. For the first time, she found herself considering an act which had always before seemed impossible—sacrificing Randall Station. Agonizing pain twisted up her body in a silent denial. The station was more than a place, it was the last living memory she had of her parents. On that land, she could imagine they were with her even today, ready to shower her with more love than she knew what to do with.

Sitting by and letting their epitaph be so cruelly cheapened was more than she could bear. And the only way to ensure its safety was to remain in this marriage that threatened to tear her to shreds.

* * *

After what had happened the previous night, Jess was simply craving peace and quiet the next morning, but a phone call altered that.

"Richard," she said, taking a seat in her studio. "Thank you so much."

"Don't thank me. You did the work." He sounded so pleased she could almost see his smile. "I loved every one of your pieces of course, but I think portraits are your strong suit."

"Yes." She liked faces, liked capturing the stories told by wrinkles and laugh lines, downturned eyes and flirtatious smiles. "They're what I enjoy the most."

"Good, because that's the element I want to build the show around." A small pause. "You have a real gift, Jess." His tone had shifted, become more intense, charm falling away to reveal the driven man who'd made a name for himself in a very competitive field. "It's true that you have some way to go in terms of the maturity of your style, but the rawness of your work right now has its own strength."

She felt less nervous now that he'd said that—wholesale praise would have been a little unbelievable coming from a man as notoriously tough as Richard Dusevic. "Strong enough for a show?"

"I wouldn't have made the offer if I'd had any doubts on that score." A statement so blunt, it could have come from Gabriel. "Your work is honest, brutally so sometimes.

"You don't hide behind affectations or polish and you don't allow your subjects to hide either. I'm going to ask you to paint me, though it scares me what you'll see."

His words triggered a precious memory.

She'd painted her mother once, a long time ago. Beth Randall had taken one look at that simple acrylic portrait and said, "Jessie, honey, you painted my soul."

If only she could see her husband as clearly, but he was colored in inky black. Opaque. Unknowable. "Where do we go from here?"

"We'll work together to select the pieces and if at any stage we don't think it's a go, we can delay it. So don't stress yourself. That's my job."

After the positive nature of that call, she felt considerably more focused, more confident. The feeling stayed with her throughout the day and by the time she sat down to dinner with Gabriel that night, she'd made up her mind to extend an olive branch. They couldn't go on this way, not with so much at stake. It was while she was in the act of bracing herself to break the silence that the phone rang again.

"It's a girl!" Damon cried. "And bloody healthy despite coming three weeks early. She doesn't even need an incubator. Man, this kid was determined to be born!"

"Congratulations." It would have taken a harder heart than hers to stop from breaking into a smile. "Have you named her?"

"Kayla's thinking it over."

"What about you?"

A few seconds of silence. "Will you come visit? Kayla said she'd like that."

Jess paused, then forged ahead. Gabe could believe what he liked—she knew what was in her heart. "Sure, I'll drive down tomorrow." It'd be an exhausting round trip, but she could use the time alone to clear her head.

"I'll be waiting."

Disturbed by the tone of that last statement, she

pressed the end button and put the receiver beside her plate. "Kayla gave birth. A healthy girl."

"I'll fly you. It'll be quicker."

She focused deliberately on the peas on her plate. "You don't have to visit."

"We'll leave at around seven."

"Fine." She chewed with single-minded focus, knowing full well why he was accompanying her. He didn't trust her even in this most innocent of situations.

Mid-morning the next day found them in the back seat of a taxi going from airport to hospital.

"You're spending a lot of time away from the station." And Angel was the most important thing in Gabriel Dumont's life.

"It's necessary."

"I wouldn't say that."

"Jess, we're not having this conversation here."

Cheeks flushing at the sharp rebuke, she turned to glance at the passing city scenery, but saw nothing. "I talked to Richard again this morning. He's thinking about scheduling the show for a month from now."

The taxi rolled to a smooth stop in front of the hospital as she finished speaking. Getting out with the flowers she'd bought at the airport, she waited for Gabe to pay the driver and walk around to join her.

"That should keep you busy," he said as they headed toward the entrance.

Her fingers squeezed the flower stems. "Like a child with a toy?" Glancing at a signboard inside the doorway, she made her way toward the elevators.

"A child is exactly what you're acting like right now." He pressed the button to go up.

The elevator opened immediately.

She stepped inside and punched the button for Kayla's floor. "Why? Because I want you to treat me and my work with some respect?"

"Respect has to be earned."

"Yes, it does."

Getting off the elevator several excruciating seconds later, they covered the remaining distance without further speech. When they entered the room, it was to discover Damon sitting beside Kayla's bed, his mouth pursed shut. So was hers. And from the looks on their faces, the silence wasn't a good one.

Jess felt like an intruder but the couple brightened at the sight of visitors. She had the disturbing feeling they'd have welcomed any interruption.

"How are you?" she asked Kayla, putting the flowers on the bedside table. "And your baby?"

The brunette's lips curved into a true smile. "She's a darling. Do you want to hold her?"

"Can I?"

"I'll bring her over," Damon offered, looking genuinely happy.

Jess's heart cried a tear of sorrow when she saw him gather the baby from the crib. As a teen, she'd dreamed such dreams—it had been Damon's child she'd expected to carry, his name she'd expected to bear.

A hand closed over her shoulder, a silent reminder of who she now belonged to. Taking a deep breath, she let Damon put his child into her arms. "Oh, she's beautiful."

"A wrinkled little nut," he said, "but she's our nut, aren't you, Cecily?"

Kayla laughed. "That's what we're calling her, Cecily Elizabeth Hart."

"I love it." Jess ran her finger over Cecily's tender skin and that quickly, her pregnancy became real in the most emotional sense of the word. In a few months' time, she too would be the nervous parent of a tiny son or daughter. Perhaps that child would have Gabriel's green eyes and her red hair. Wouldn't that be something?

Feeling a sense of intimacy with Gabe that overcame all their disagreements, she turned to him with a smile. "Would you like to hold her?"

His jaw set in a hard line. "No." It was a quiet but brutal denial that didn't reach Cecily's parents, both of whom were involved in resettling a pillow that had slipped from Kayla's back.

Her eyes widened. She couldn't believe Gabe had turned so cold over this blameless child. She'd always believed that while her husband might be harsh, he'd never be needlessly cruel.

But now she had evidence otherwise.

Attempting to come to grips with this unexpected and unwelcome facet of his personality, she put Cecily into her mother's waiting arms. "She's perfect." A touch of nausea hit her as she rose from handing over the baby. She had to take several deep breaths to get past it.

Kayla gave her a measuring look before turning to Damon. "Do you think you could get me one of those fizzy orange juices from the vending machine down the hall?"

"Yeah, okay." Damon glanced across at Gabriel. "I owe you for the other night. Let me buy you a coffee." His voice was tense but polite. "I think the machine does a less than awful imitation."

To her surprise, Gabriel accepted the offer. Kayla waited only until the men's footsteps had died away to blurt out, "You're pregnant, aren't you?"

"Do you have radar?" Jess gaped.

"Must be the hormones." She kissed Cecily's forehead. "How do you feel?"

"In love with him or her, already." That had become truth mere minutes ago. And it caused a new worry to loom large—if Gabe truly was heartless enough to react so negatively to an infant, what kind of a father would he be? Too late she came to the awful realization that she'd put her baby's happiness on the line along with her own when she'd walked into this marriage.

"I was the same." Kayla paused, her smile slipping. "Can we be friends, Jess?"

Surprised at the non-sequitor, Jess nodded. "We already are."

"No, you don't understand." Sighing, the brunette hugged Cecily to her chest. "I don't know if I can save my marriage with you around."

The implied accusation hit her like a punch to the jaw. "I'd never break my marriage vows or ask Damon to break his."

"I know. I don't think that of you. Really. But seeing you reminds him of…of what he gave up." Her eyes were huge. "I've asked him to move away from Kowhai, maybe up to Hawkes Bay. I have family there and he could easily find work, what with the orchards and all."

Jess hated that she was the cause of another woman's unhappiness, even if that same woman had once driven a stake right through her heart. Things had changed since then, become far less black and white. "I hope you two make it."

Damon walked in the very next second. He put the can of juice beside the flowers on the beside table. "Here you go. Gabe's grabbing you a coffee, too," he told Jess, an edge to his voice that she understood all too well and which made her incredibly angry. He was speaking in front of his wife for God's sake.

"So, what have you two been talking about?"

Kayla smiled. "It looks like congratulations are in order for Jess and Gabe."

Jess felt her stomach drop but the other woman was too excited at sharing the news to notice anything wrong.

"She's going to have a baby, too!"

Damon's face went blank for a frozen second before he recovered. "Hey, that's really something."

"What is?" Gabe's voice came from the doorway. "Jess." He held out a cup of takeout coffee. "It's not too bad."

She walked over and took the coffee, hoping against hope that something would happen to interrupt the inevitable. "Oh it's—" she began, but Damon was already speaking.

"The baby." He smiled and Jess could tell it was forced. And if she could tell, then so could her husband. "You must be really happy."

Twelve

Jess knew the second Gabe understood. She'd been leaning slightly into him and now felt the muscles in his body go as taut as high-tension wire. But when he spoke, there was no indication of surprise in his tone. "Nothing in the world quite like it. But you'd know that."

Damon nodded. "Yeah."

"We'd better get going." Jess needed to get out of here and fix this mess. If it could be fixed. The single good thing that could be said was that neither Kayla nor Damon appeared to have any inkling of what had really just happened. "Things are getting busy at the station."

"Thanks for coming." Kayla smiled, but her eyes were on Damon as he came to hug Jess.

"If you ever need me," he took the chance to whisper.

Calling on his strength was no longer her right. Nor did she covet it. "Take care of your family, Damon."

And then she turned and walked away with the man who was now supposed to be her strength. Except that he was far too hard, far too untouchable.

Clear blue sky spread out in front of the plane, but the air was decidedly stormy inside. "Aren't you going to say anything?" Jess finally asked several minutes into the flight.

"What would you like me to say?"

"I'm sorry. So, so sorry. Kayla guessed and then she told Damon."

He looked at her, the green of his eyes clouded by the darkest fury she'd ever seen. "Why didn't *you* tell me?"

"I needed time to get used to the idea." She hated how hollow that sounded, though it was at least half the truth. Still, it was hardly enough to justify what had happened. "I never thought anybody would figure it out before I told you."

Instead of releasing his anger at her, something she would have fully understood, he didn't say another word on the subject. The next week passed in the same near-silence. When they spoke, it was about nothing important, and in bed, the solitary sounds were those of his demands and her whispered pleasures.

Or of her crying out his name.

Ever since that lie she'd thrown at him in anger, he always made her say his name, made her remember whose arms she was in. As if she could forget.

Jess knew it wasn't just her pregnancy they had to talk about, but also how Gabe had treated Cecily in the hospital. But she couldn't do it, simply could not bring herself to shatter her last illusions about this man she'd married for all the wrong reasons. So she threw herself into her work. However even her beloved art failed as a tool to keep her from thinking.

And the reason for that was terrifying. Despite her repeated admonitions to herself to never forget that theirs was a marriage based on business, not love, she'd somehow begun to think of Gabriel as her husband in more than name only, begun to accept him on a level that went far below the surface.

That night when he'd gone with her to help Kayla and Damon had altered how she viewed him. The change had been coming bit by slow bit but that one act had truly pushed aside her preconceptions about who he was. Now she wasn't sure she hadn't merely replaced one illusion with another.

Tapping her pencil on top of the sketch pad, she stared at the beautiful mare nickering at her from over the stall gate. "I wish I could get on you and ride away into the sunset." Just run away from her problems. But the thing was, she'd done that once already. And if she still wasn't strong enough to deal with her life, then that year in L.A. had been a total waste.

Which brought her back to the endless circle of her confused thoughts. Gabriel was the one who'd sent her to L.A. on the faith of her promise that she'd be back. He'd let her go, given her what she wanted. Did that make him a good man, or simply one calculating enough to play the odds and ensure he came out the winner? After all, that year of freedom had left her even further indebted to him.

Jess didn't know the answer…to anything. Least of all her own emotional turmoil. Frustrated, she began to draw. Page after page after page, stroke after stroke, capturing every inch of the stables and the two horses currently in it. The hours passed. And at last, she was able to stop thinking and simply *be*.

Gabriel was talking to Jim about some repairs to the quarters where the shearing gang stayed when they came around each season to strip the sheep of their woolly coats. However his concentration was shot, anger tearing holes through his focus and deflecting his attention toward the stables…toward Jess. "What?" he said, when Jim seemed to be waiting for a response.

"You okay, Gabe?"

No. Right now all he could think about was the distant way Jess had been acting since that day at the hospital. He could well guess why—Damon had told him about his and Kayla's planned move.

Surprised at the depth of his own anger at Jess's inability to get over the younger man, Gabe had made no move to bridge that distance. Except at night. And then he'd made very sure that *he* was the only man on her mind. "Why don't we discuss this another time? The maintenance isn't urgent."

Jim raised an eyebrow. "Sure. Not like you're listening to me anyway."

"Sorry."

"Good thing I don't offend easy." He grinned. "The quarters can wait, but we do have to talk about whether or not to start break feeding."

Break feeding involved putting the ewes into a defined area much smaller than their usual pastures until they denuded that section of grass. It slowed their weight gain, a necessity since overweight ewes sometimes had trouble lambing.

Gabriel forced himself to think. "Let's hold off on that for a week."

"Yeah, that's what I was thinking, too." The foreman raised his head at a call from one of the hands. "Gotta go. Oh wait, I forgot to tell you—one of the farm bikes died for good yesterday. We need to get it replaced."

"It's already on the way along with a spare." He'd put in the order after conferring with the station mechanic last month. "Should be here within the week." A delighted wave later, Jim was gone, but Gabe stood staring at the ground for several minutes before giving himself a mental kick and getting moving.

He had a hundred things to do, including checking the southern access road for damaged gates. That was all he needed right now-stock escaping out onto a road used by heavily laden trucks among other vehicles. Kowhai was fine for small purchases, but the bulk of their supplies were delivered, either by truck or by air. Which reminded him—he needed to talk to one of the contractors about some additions to the usual delivery.

Frowning in thought, he lifted his head just in time to see smoke puff out from the stables. A lick of flame followed. His heart stopped.

Jess was in there.

Everything else was wiped from his mind, his sole thought to get her out. Alive. He didn't stop to give instructions to the men—there was a detailed system in place on Angel in case of fire. Gabriel had been accused of being obsessive about the drills, but today, the men reacted with military precision. The fire wouldn't be allowed to spread. However that wouldn't save Jess if she'd already been overcome by the smoke.

One of the horses burst out in a rush of terror as

Gabe ran inside. Coughing against the smoke, he refused to consider that Jess might've been crushed under the hooves of the panicked animal.

The fire was far worse than it looked from the outside, the stored hay going up like paper. "Jess!" He had no idea where she'd been when the fire broke out, but went with instinct and headed toward the two stalls that had been occupied today. If he knew his wife, she would have tried to save the animals. "Jess! Jessica!"

Eyes burning, he lowered his body in an effort to get under the smoke. The sound of violent neighing alerted him that the other horse remained trapped. A second later, he found both the horse and Jess. She was attempting to lead the animal out but it was too frightened to cooperate, kicking and rearing back from the flames licking up the opposite wall.

Tears streamed down his wife's face but he knew she'd never even considered leaving the horse behind.

"Jess!"

Seeing him, she mouthed his name. Every protective impulse he had punched through to the surface, screaming at him to get her out. Taking the reins from her, he pushed her forward. "Go!"

She didn't argue. He got the horse moving and headed in the same direction, only to bump into her as she stood bent over, body wracked by coughs. Decision made in a split-second, he set the horse free and slapped its rump. It ran instinctively toward the freedom it could sense in the slight wind blowing through the doors.

Gabe took Jess into his arms. His lungs were on fire and his scarred arm seemed to burn anew, as if the skin remembered its decades-old ordeal. Gritting his teeth, he fought off the memories and followed the sound trail laid by the horse. They'd wrenched back his struggling body when he'd tried to save his family but he *was* going to get Jess out.

Not allowing himself to think of anything else, he focused on locating the entrance. Then there it was—a gate out of hell. Cold air rushed into his lungs as he staggered out. Someone tried to take Jess from him but he refused to release her until he was sure she'd survived unscathed. Her hand touched his cheek. "I'm okay." The words came out as a croak but they proved to be what he needed to hear.

Several hours later, Jess went looking for her husband. Dr. Mackey had checked her out and declared what she already knew—she was fine. He didn't think the baby had been harmed, but had in his practical way, pointed out that she was barely pregnant. If her baby was strong, it'd make it. Jess had preferred hearing that over platitudes. She also had every faith in her child. Half its genes were Dumont and those were nothing if not stubborn.

She found Gabe near the smoldering ruins. The stables had been gutted, but none of the other buildings had suffered any damage due to the quick action of the men and women on the station. "They did good," she said, walking up to stand beside him.

"What are you doing up?" He scowled, the brim of his hat shadowing the expression to dark intensity. "You were supposed to rest."

"Dr. Mackey said nothing about that." She coughed to clear a slightly husky throat. "You're the one who decided I should play invalid."

"What happened in there?" He turned to face her, hands on his hips.

Paradoxically, the aggressive posture calmed her. She'd worried the fire might have awakened bad memories, but from what she could see, he was his usual abrasive self. "I don't know. I fell asleep."

"You what?" It was almost a growl.

"I spent the night throwing up," she told him in case he hadn't heard her lurching about.

"So you fell asleep in the *stables?*"

She scowled. "What's wrong with you? No one got hurt, the horses are okay."

He took a long, deep breath, as if trying to calm himself. "Where did you fall asleep?"

"What does it matter?" She really couldn't see why he was getting so worked up about this.

"Where?" he snapped.

"Where do you think? On one of the haybales. It was there and I was getting drowsy so I just laid down." Nothing out of the extraordinary.

"You were on hay." He sounded so in control, it told her exactly how angry he was. "You could've been killed."

"I woke up when the horses started kicking the walls. There was time for me to open up the stalls, but Starr wouldn't leave."

"So you decided to risk your neck to save hers."

"I couldn't leave her there." She could not believe he was arguing with her over this. She'd seen the way he cared for the station animals. "She was completely panicked."

"You should've got the hell out the second you knew something had gone wrong."

"Why?"

"Why?" He looked as though he wanted to strangle

her. "Because you know how fast hay burns and the building was wood for crissakes!"

A twinge of conscience pinched her because he was right. If he hadn't come in after her, she could have been in serious trouble. But something in her wouldn't let her admit that. "I had to get the horses out." She had a sudden thought. "I'm fine, Gabe. Really. And the baby will be, too."

"I have trained men for emergencies. They could've rescued Starr and with less fuss."

The ice in his eyes put paid to her silly notion that he was acting this way because he'd been frightened for her safety. "Pardon me for having a heart. Maybe if I was like you," she said without thinking, "I would have been able to leave that poor horse in there!"

He'd opened his mouth to respond when Jim walked up and spoke in his ear. His entire face went so dangerously quiet that she knew they'd located the person responsible for the fire.

"Send him to my office." The words were ground out.

Jess waited until the foreman had left before asking, "What happened?"

"I'll deal with it."

She fell in step with him as he strode toward the house. "Then you won't mind if I watch."

"This is station business." He walked in the door.

"Wives help with station business."

"You're not that sort of wife." It was a cutting declaration. "I don't want or need your interference."

She narrowed her eyes. The man was deliberately attempting to make her angry so she'd leave. It made her wonder how many other times she'd fallen for the same act. "Too bad."

"Suit yourself. Don't get in the way." Throwing his hat onto the study desk, he thrust a hand through his hair and remained in a standing position.

A young man appeared in the doorway a bare minute later. Jess had never seen anyone look more terrified. She knew him. Corey had been in the stables earlier and had admired her sketches. She couldn't imagine how he was involved.

"Close the door."

Corey did as asked but stayed as far from Gabe as physically possible. She didn't blame him—Gabe's calm was so deadly, even she was scared. And she knew he'd never harm a hair on her head.

"You have a minute to convince me I shouldn't call the police."

Corey's face threatened to crumple for a second. But to his credit, he squared his shoulders and looked Gabe straight in the eye. "It wasn't intentional, sir." He swallowed. "I was smoking. I dropped a stub and thought I'd crushed it out. But—but that's where they say the fire started so it must not have been out."

Jess saw Gabe's hands turn into fists. Her stomach dropped. Then they opened and she breathed a sigh of relief, belatedly realizing that she'd been way off base about how badly the fire had affected him. She'd never seen him like this, so close to the edge it was frightening.

"How long have you worked here?" he asked and his voice was a whip.

"A year, sir."

"And in that year, did you learn the rules?"

Corey's head dropped. "Yes, sir."

"Maybe you'd like to tell me what the first rule is."

"No smoking on Angel. Anywhere on Angel."

Jess hadn't known that, but now that she thought about it, she'd never seen a single hand with a cigarette hanging from his lips. And that was unusual. Around here, a lot of the men didn't care about lung cancer or second-hand smoke. They had far more to fear from the land itself.

"You're fired." Gabe's jaw was granite. "Get the hell off the property and don't show your face ever again."

She'd expected Corey to bolt, but to her surprise, he held his ground. "I'm sorry, sir." He looked toward her. "Mrs. Dumont, I never meant to hurt you."

"I know you didn't," Jess said but knew she couldn't intervene.

"Sir, if you—" Corey broke off as Gabe's expression seemed to harden even more. Taking a halting breath, he restarted. "If you kick me off Angel, no one else will hire me."

Jess knew the boy wasn't lying. The station owners around here might not always agree with each other, but on certain things they were a wall.

Gabe didn't respond to the plea.

Corey rubbed his hands on his thighs. "I need the work."

"Get out. I won't ask again."

Shoulders slumped, Corey left the room.

Jess waited until he was gone to walk over and put a hand on Gabe's arm. "Gabe, I want—"

"I said no interference, Jess. Don't you dare plead his case."

She straightened her spine. "Why not? Because you're too blinded by the past to listen?"

White lines bracketed his mouth. "How I run this station is my business."

"Yeah, well you made it mine, too, when you married me. And you'll listen to what I have to say."

"Or what?" he said, quiet and dangerous. "You won't sleep with me?"

Thirteen

That was one place she wasn't going to go. "He has a three-year-old girl. Her mother ran off leaving him with the baby when Corey was sixteen."

Finally, a hint of something other than anger appeared in Gabe's eyes. "And you know this because?"

"Because he showed me her picture and asked if I could do a sketch of her sometime." It had broken her heart to see the love in his eyes. "He took responsibility for his child but he dropped out of school to do it. Station work is all he knows. You cut him off and he's got no other options."

Gabe's expression closed down again. "He knew the rules and he broke them. He's lucky I didn't have him charged."

"But—" She tightened her grip on his arm.

"Leave, Jess. I need to start the insurance paperwork." And that coldly, he shook off her hand and went around the desk to his chair.

Jess felt something fragile inside her break, something tender and newly formed. "I thought you were…. But you've got no more heart than a block of stone."

Gabe heard the door slam behind Jess. It reverberated through his bones.

…*no more heart than a block of stone.*

She was right. He'd been ten years old when emotion had been seared out of him by the brutal deaths of his family and he had no intention of ever letting it back in. Not for Jess. Not for anyone. She'd known that when she married him, so why did she seem so damn surprised?

Refusing to give in to the urge to punch something or someone, he picked up the phone and dialed a familiar number. "Sam?" He silenced the part of his mind that asked him why he was doing this.

"Hi, Gabe." Sam's voice was without pretension, though he owned one of the most lucrative vineyards in Marlborough. "What's up?"

"I need a favor."

Jess was so angry at Gabe that she locked both the doors leading to her bedroom. Despite their troubles to date, it was the first time she'd done that. She knew he'd think she was making the power play he'd accused her of, using sex as a bargaining tool.

But the truth was both far simpler and far more complex. Not only had she not forgotten his treatment of Cecily, she now had further evidence of his inhumanity in his inability to forgive Corey. And she couldn't imagine sleeping with a man capable of such cruelty.

A knot formed in her throat. She agreed Corey had made a mistake and a bad one at that, but surely everyone deserved a second chance? However Gabe was the one with the power. And he'd thrown Corey out without a single thought. What made it worse was that she hadn't been able to tell whether his action was rooted in decades-old pain, or simple cold-hearted vengeance.

Tears trickled down her face. Stupid, impractical tears. Even when she thought she had no illusions left, Gabe did something that splintered one and she realized she'd been clutching onto yet another dream that could never be. Her hand went to her stomach. Once again, she wondered what kind of a father he'd be. If he could condemn Corey so very easily, mightn't he one day turn on his own child because that child had broken the rules?

The scenario was excruciatingly easy to imagine. And it hurt. Gabe had always had the ability to wound her with his ruthless practicality, but she'd been able to bear that, cushioned by a layer of distance…by her love for Damon.

But that cushion was no longer there. And she was too terrified to ask herself why. All she knew was that Gabriel now had a direct line to her most vulnerable self, a truth she couldn't ever let him know, not a man so harsh as he'd proven today.

She fell asleep with that thought buzzing through her brain. When she woke, it was already far too late. Gabriel was carrying her to his bed and her arms were wrapped around his neck, her body betraying her even in sleep.

"What are you doing?"

"Taking you back where you belong." He sat on his bed with her in his lap.

She put a hand on his bare chest. "What if I don't want to be here?"

His answer was to kiss her, kiss her until her world spun and he became her sole anchor. She clung to him as she would to a life raft in a storm, his body muscular and powerful, protective and safe. But, of course, that was yet another illusion.

Breaking the kiss, she looked into that pitiless masculine face. Her pulse pounded in every inch of her skin. "I don't like you very much right now."

The blunt honesty didn't faze him. "That doesn't matter. You still want me." Sliding his hand up her thigh, he began to kiss the vulnerable line of her neck.

She sucked in a breath and tried to push him away. But he cupped her with that big, rough hand that knew her needs so well. It was all she could do not to cry out. "That's—that's n-not how it should be."

He turned to place her on the bed, removing his hand so he could brace his body over hers. His next kiss was coaxing…gentle. Except it allowed no escape, wrapping her up in a cocoon of sexuality as real and as powerful as the man holding her prisoner. "We have passion. That's enough."

Fighting through the sensual haze, she found herself saying something she knew she shouldn't. "What about love?" It came out as a whisper so soft, she wondered if he'd heard.

He tangled his lower body with hers. "Love is for fools."

Those were the last words spoken by either of them as their bodies took up the conversation in a turbulent storm of hunger and unspoken need. Jess was drowning in what Gabe could do to her, but even in the midst of her pleasure, something struck her as different.

He'd never ever hurt her in bed, but tonight there was a carefulness, an aching tenderness to his touch that was new. He spent hours going over every inch of her skin, not letting her hurry him, no matter how she urged. In the end, she surrendered to that strange tenderness and it was another irrevocable step into the unknown.

After the haunting beauty of his lovemaking that night, Jess expected *some* change in their relationship, perhaps a new honesty born out of those intimacies. But even as she readied herself to face that change, hours turned into days and Gabe seemed to withdraw further and further from her.

It was true that she was busy preparing for the show, and he had to handle the rebuilding of the stables on top of the approaching lambing season, but notwithstanding all that, they seemed to connect less and less as the days passed.

That in itself might not have alarmed her if she hadn't begun to notice that Gabe refused to discuss the baby. At first, he was too busy to accompany her to the doctor's when she went for a check-up. She didn't pay much mind to that—he was hardly the kind of man who'd insist on following the pregnancy every step of the way.

But he became distant every time she brought up the topic—he never asked questions of his own volition. Part of her thought it was all in her imagination, what with the pregnancy seeming to turn her into a walking explosion of hormones. Another bigger part of her was convinced something was seriously wrong. However attempting to bring it up with Gabe was like trying to run uphill against the wind.

Days passed and still she didn't push. Things were relatively smooth between them and she didn't want to make ripples, especially not when all she had were the very vaguest of misgivings. Their relationship might have gone on in this way for months if she hadn't picked up the business line one night.

"Angel Station." She sipped her coffee, her mind on the show which was only a week away. Another important date loomed much closer, falling this coming Saturday in point of fact. And Gabe hadn't said a word about it so far.

"Jess, is that you?" The voice was feminine, slightly husky and amused. "Acting as Gabe's secretary now?"

The coffee suddenly tasted like dust. "Hi, Sylvie. What can I do for you?"

"Actually, I needed to talk to Gabe about something." She paused. "Well, I'm sure you know, with the anniversary approaching."

Jess's hand squeezed the receiver. "It was nice of you to call."

"I couldn't not call, could I? I mean not many people know the truth. Oh, I suppose you do, don't you?"

Jess knew full well the other woman was being purposefully bitchy, but she couldn't help the hurt that sliced through her. The fact was that Sylvie was only able to do what she was doing because of Gabe. He'd made the decision to keep his wife in the dark about everything that mattered.

Gabriel returned at that moment. "Hold on, Sylvie. Gabe's here." Passing him the receiver, she took her coffee and walked out. This time she ignored the dangerous temptation to listen in and went to sit on the back steps. The stars sparkled bright overhead but she barely noticed them. It was hard to see beauty through the dull ache of an angry hurt.

She didn't move even when she heard Gabriel's footsteps a few minutes later. He sat behind her, his legs on either side of her body, the heat of his chest pressed to her back. But he couldn't warm the cold places in her heart.

"What did Sylvie say to you?"

Unsurprised by the question, she put down her coffee and wrapped her arms around herself. "Don't worry. She didn't tell me your secrets." She focused on the farthest star she could see on the horizon, a bright pinprick that offered hope even in the darkest of times.

A cruel lie.

Sometimes darkness was all there was.

Gabriel ran one hand down her arm. "Sylvie and—"

"I don't want to know." She could live her whole life without knowing about his relationship with Sylvie. "She's nothing to me. But you're my husband and I'd like very much to know what that means."

"Jess." A quiet warning.

"Food, shelter, sex." She ticked off the elements one by one, her voice outwardly serene though a strange fury roared in her blood. "The basic three. Oh wait, I forgot—a baby. You gave me that, too. But you don't seem to want that baby very much."

"I'll provide for our child."

"Like you provide for me?" she snapped. "Or like you provide for Sylvie?"

"We've had this conversation before."

"I don't think you're cheating, Gabe. At least not with your body." Shaking off his touch, she stood and turned to face him. "But what do you call it when you tell her things you don't tell me?"

He didn't rise but anger threaded his voice. "Isn't that the pot calling the kettle black?"

"Okay, yes, I messed up. I should've told you about the baby straightaway instead of letting you find out from Damon."

"Very generous of you." Sarcasm laced every syllable.

"Don't reduce this to a petty squabble." She shook her head. "It's important." The silence ended today, no matter that it would splinter the calm of their relationship. In truth, she'd always known it was a false calm, hiding more than it revealed.

"I walked into this marriage with my eyes wide open." She thumped a fist against her chest. "I married you despite knowing what kind of a man you were. But our child didn't make that choice. So I don't care how much you confide in Sylvie," she lied, "or how much you ignore me, or that you treat me like a convenience, but you are not hurting our child like that. You will give our baby the love and respect he, or she, deserves!"

He finally rose to his feet. "Are you finished?"

"No, I'm not." She was too angry to be intimidated by his size. "I'm never going to be finished on this topic. You wanted a wife and a child, but that means you have to be a husband and a father. You know what, forget the hell about being a decent husband—just concentrate on being a good father."

"I don't want to be a father."

Stunned, thinking she'd misheard, she froze. "What?"

"I made a mistake when I asked you to get pregnant."

The words fell between them like drops of icy rain.

Jess couldn't accept what had been said. "Are you asking me to…" She put a protective hand on her abdomen.

"Of course not. I'm not a monster." His face was a

shadow in the darkness. "But don't expect me to be some doting father either. I'll support the child but I want it in boarding school the second it's old enough."

Every part of her rejected that idea. "What is wrong with you?" she yelled. "This is our baby you're talking about, not an unwanted piece of furniture."

"I mean what I say." His tone was pure steel. "That kid is not staying in this house a moment longer than necessary."

A horrible thought crept into her mind. "Do you really think I cheated on you?" she whispered. "Is that what this is about? You think it's not your child?"

Fourteen

"Don't be stupid, Jess. I know I'm as responsible for it as you."

"Responsibility? *It?* We're talking about our baby, Gabriel!" she repeated, reaching out to grip his arms and shake him, but he was immoveable. "How can you single-handedly decide you're going to send our child away?"

"That's the end of this discussion." He pushed her hands off his arms, gentle but firm.

Shaken to the core, she stood unmoving as he turned to walk inside the house. And then she knew, as if an angel had whispered the answer in her ear. "This is about them."

He faced her. "It's about nothing but my own recognition of having made a mistake. I don't want a child underfoot and I don't want to be a father."

"The fact that the anniversary of the fire is two days away has nothing to do with it?"

"I got used to that a long time ago. It's just another day." The door slammed behind him.

Jess sat on the step, hugging her arms around her raised knees. She had no idea what to do. Gabriel had sounded so resolute, so unyielding.

But tempting as it was to take the easy route, she hadn't lost the ability to think. Not yet. The anniversary *was* two days away and whatever it was that Gabe didn't want her to know, it had to do with the fire and his family. What was also true was that his new attitude toward the pregnancy made no sense.

Jess rubbed at her eyes as she stood and prepared to return to the house. There had to be a reason behind his inexplicable reaction. There had to be. Because if there wasn't, then there was no hope for this marriage.

None at all.

In spite of what he'd said two nights ago when he'd dropped that bombshell about their child, Jess had expected some sort of acknowledgment of the anniversary from Gabriel. But he went about his business as usual and the others on the station followed his lead.

"Is it always like this?" she asked Mrs. C., feeling disloyal for making even that simple inquiry.

"Long as I've been working here." The other woman put away the lunch dishes. "Don't fuss so, Jess. He was a young boy when it happened. It's natural he'd put it behind him."

Jess wondered exactly how well he'd put it behind him. She was sure he'd had another nightmare last night. After a few more minutes of useless thinking, she picked up the keys to the SUV. "I'm going to the Randall station house," she made sure to tell Mrs. C. "I want to do some work on the garden, but I'll be back before dark."

"I'll let Gabe know." Mrs. C. smiled. "Do you want to take a snack with you?"

"Have you got some crackers or something?"

Mrs. C. eventually sent her on her way with far too much food, including a container of fresh fruit salad and a thermos full of the hot, sweet tea Jess had taken to drinking lately. Driving out, Jess wondered if she should've told Mrs. C the real reason for her journey but decided she'd done the right thing. Anyone looking for her would find her easily enough.

The drive from Angel to what had once been her home was now familiar. She got out without feeling the least bit tired and spent the next hour tidying up the garden. Then, using a pair of gardening shears, she began to gather a large bunch of flowers from the plants that had anticipated the coming spring. Because she didn't want to denude any one area, it took her almost half an hour to collect a sizable bouquet.

Putting the mass on the passenger seat, she drove to the Randall family plot to lay some blooms on her parents' graves. "I miss you," she said quietly. "But I think I'm going to be okay now. Funny how such a tiny thing inside you can make you so strong."

Returning to the car after a quick tidy up of the area, she turned back toward Angel. The Dumont plot was located about fifteen minutes from the main house.

When she arrived, she was surprised to find one of the small flatbed trucks used around the station parked nearby. Who else, she wondered, had come to pay their respects? Bringing the SUV to a stop, she got out, grabbed the flowers and made her way around the truck. But the man she saw kneeling by a heartbreakingly small headstone was not anyone she'd expected.

Feeling like a trespasser on his grief, she would have left had he not already seen her. "I bought flowers."

There was no visible sadness on Gabriel's face. But three of the graves had little gifts on them—a pinecone on the first, a river-stone on the second and a tiny bunch of wild daisies on the third. Swallowing her tears, she added her offerings to his while he stood by, a silent shadow.

"I'm sorry." She met those impenetrable green eyes. "I didn't mean to intrude."

"There's nothing to be sorry about." He dusted off his hat and placed it on his head. "I have to be getting back."

And that quickly, he was gone. But she wasn't fooled, not this time. Turning, she looked at those graves again. Daisies for a tiny sister who'd probably made daisy chains, a river-stone for Raphael—maybe he'd liked to fish or swim—and a pinecone for Michael who'd perhaps loved to climb.

Such small things and yet Gabriel had gone to the trouble of finding and bringing them here. Crying openly, she began to head back to the SUV. Then something made her turn and look at the two adult graves. Nothing lay on them but the flowers she'd put there.

There was no longer any doubt in her mind that Gabriel had loved his siblings deeply, but those two barren graves told her that that wasn't the only part of this story she'd gotten wrong. What had happened with Stephen and Mary Dumont? And why was her husband still so angry about it?

Angry enough to forsake his own child.

* * *

Jess spent the next several days trying to get Gabriel to talk and hitting a brick wall. Their battles were so intense and his silence so intractable that by the time she landed in Auckland for the show, she was emotionally black and blue. He'd shut her out to a degree that frightened her, making her despair for the future of their marriage.

"Jess!"

She jerked up at the sound of her own name and met Mrs. Kilpatrick's excited face. "Thanks for coming to pick me up."

Mrs. Kilpatrick enveloped her in a hug scented with Chanel No.5. "Think nothing of it. Since I was already here and with the car, it was no problem. I'm so delighted for you. Richard's generated lots of advance buzz for the opening so I'm sure it'll be a smash."

"I have a feeling you had a lot to do with that, too." Jess had a very good idea of Mrs. Kilpatrick's social reach.

The other woman brushed off the words but a pleased blush lit up her features. "Let's get you to the hotel. It's eleven now so you'll have plenty of time to get ready for the opening. Richard did tell you he decided to push it back to seven?"

"Yes." Jess nodded, though she felt curiously detached from the whole thing.

"What about Gabriel? Is he taking a later flight, or flying himself up?" Mrs. Kilpatrick unlocked the trunk of her rental car and Jess put in her small case.

"He isn't going to make it." She tried not to betray her disappointment. "He's so busy right now."

"Oh, that's unfortunate but I do know how it gets."

The drive from the airport to the hotel passed by easily enough and Jess was in her room within the hour.

Soon after that came lunch at the hotel restaurant, where she met Richard for the first time.

He was as charming and as intelligent in person as he'd been over the phone and on e-mail. She found her trust in his judgment solidifying into genuine liking. A feeling that he apparently shared if his farewell comment was anything to go by.

"My dear, sweet Jess, I think we're going to have a long and exciting relationship." Smiling, he gave her a kiss on the cheek. "Having a chance to nurture a talent like yours is what makes me have faith in my work."

The compliment boosted her professional confidence, but emotionally, she continued to feel off-kilter. Lost. "Thank you."

When he left to finalize things at the gallery, she went back up to her room and hung out the dress she planned to squeeze into for the opening. The *red* dress, rich as wine and dark as blood. It was already almost too snug with the way her body was changing, so this would be her last chance to wear it for a while. And wear it she would. Too bad if her husband couldn't be bothered to show up.

After popping out for a quick shopping trip to pick up some things she couldn't get in Kowhai, she returned to get ready, as Richard wanted her at the gallery an hour early. The phone came to life a minute into her preparations, making her heart stutter. Maybe Gabe had changed his mind.

"Hello?"

"Jessie, guess where I am?"

The dawning smile was wiped off her face. "Damon." She sat on the bed. "Aren't you supposed to be in Hawkes Bay?"

"I was but I called home last night and heard you

were having a show. I couldn't miss my Jessie's first show. My mom called someone and they called Mrs. Kilpatrick and now I'm on the guest list." He chuckled. "I'm in Hamilton right now, should make it to Auckland before your party starts."

"What about Kayla and Cecily?"

"They're at home. Kayla didn't want to drive up with the baby."

"Of course she didn't. Cecily's too young for such a long drive."

A pause. "I thought you'd be happy. We haven't had a chance to see each other since the hospital."

"You have a wife and a child, Damon." She wondered if he was hearing what she was trying to say. "Get back in that car and go home to them or maybe Kayla will stop waiting for you."

"Like you, Jess?" The volume of his voice dropped. "Have you stopped waiting for me?"

She squeezed her eyes shut. "I'll always be your friend."

"I sure screwed up when I let you go."

"No, you didn't." He could have never made her happy, something she'd finally begun to understand. "You married a woman who loves you and you have a beautiful daughter. Don't throw that away."

Another pause. "I guess I got selfish, wanting to be loved by you, too. But that's gone isn't it?"

"Yes," she said. "It's gone." She wasn't sure it had ever really existed. And that scared her, because for her to question what had once been an absolute truth meant that something far more powerful had taken its place. Something stronger, more enduring and infinitely more real than the fading illusion of a teenage dream. "You take care of your family, Damon."

"And you be careful, Jessie. He's not—"

"Shh." She shook her head—some loyalties were set in stone. "Have a safe trip home."

He didn't bring up the subject again. "I hope you become rich and famous."

Hanging up, Jess dove back into her interrupted preparations. If she didn't think about what had just occurred, about her devastating insight into the nature of her feelings for Damon, she wouldn't have to consider the reason behind it…wouldn't have to look into the vibrant heart of an emotion so raw and potent, it eclipsed everything that had come before.

Jess walked into the gallery feeling like an imposter. Taking off her coat to hang on the coatrack, she caught a glimpse of herself in the mirror hanging near the entrance. The color of the dress went beautifully with her hair, but it was the way the fabric hugged her body that was truly extraordinary.

She should have felt sexy and confident, yet she couldn't help but think that the man she most wanted to see her wasn't going to be here tonight. She wasn't important enough for him to bother. Pain cut rivers into a heart she'd tried so desperately to harden.

"Jess!" Richard's face lit up the second he saw her. "You look ravishing." He offered her his arm.

She let him lead her into the gallery space. "Should I have tried for a more arty look?" All three of his assistants were wearing head-to-toe black, though Richard himself was dressed in a beautiful dove-gray suit.

"Affectations like those," he whispered under his breath, "will make you blend in. And you, Jess, are meant to be a star." Releasing her arm, he settled her unbound hair carefully around her shoulders. "Did I tell you that it's a by-invitation-only shindig tonight? No starving art students who're just here to eat."

Her laughter came from the same part of her that couldn't seem to stop believing in hope. "How much are you asking for my paintings?"

"Lots."

"Will people pay that for an unknown?"

"They'll do as I say." His eyes gleamed. "I'm offering them a chance to get in at the bottom floor with someone I predict will become huge, and I've never been wrong."

Jess expected his prediction to buoy her up, but even when the guests started arriving and more compliments began flowing, she felt strangely disconnected. Her body might be in Auckland, but her mind was in the Mackenzie Country. The reason why wasn't something she particularly wanted to consider.

She'd just managed to extricate herself from a chatty young couple when Richard slid an arm around her waist. "If you're in the market for a rich old husband to fund your work, Mr. Matthews thinks you're a walking work of art."

"Tell Mr. Matthews that this work of art is taken."

Jess froze at the sound of that deep male voice, hardly aware of Richard's arm slipping away. And then it was being replaced by a harder, more muscular one. Everything in her thrilled to life.

Fifteen

Richard took a step back. "Jess, honey, tell the gorgeous shark by your side that I was joking."

Snapped out of her semi-shocked state, she smiled. "Richard, meet my husband, Gabriel."

Gabe's hand moved on her hip and she bit back a responsive gasp. "Richard."

She stood by while the men shook hands, her heart melting. She forgave Gabe everything—he'd come to support her despite having had made it clear that he was far too busy to do so. Surely that could only mean one thing.

"I see a potential sale over there." Beaming, Richard excused himself.

Jess shifted to face Gabe without breaking his hold. "You came." That was when she noticed the rigid angle to his jaw, the tension in the body pressed against hers. Her smile faded.

"What are you doing, Jess?" Something close to disappointment threaded through the anger. "Where is he?"

"Who?" Hope ebbed out of her drop by slow drop.

His expression grew darker. "Kayla is hysterical. She called me begging that I ask you not to take her husband."

She felt her face blanch. "I guess that answers the question of why you bothered to show up," she whispered, so hurt that she was numb.

"Jess, my dear." Mrs. Kilpatrick's voice was a welcome benediction. "Can I steal you away from your husband? I want to talk to you about a possible commission."

"Of course." She grabbed the opportunity to move out of Gabriel's hold. But no matter the lack of physical contact, she was aware of him on the most visceral level.

Time passed and she managed to avoid him till almost the end, when she found herself drifting to stand in front of a piece bearing a Not for Sale sign. It was a meticulously detailed painting of Randall Station, one of the few landscapes on show.

"Home," Gabe said from behind her, reading the title. "But home is somewhere else now, isn't it?"

"No. Home is a place of safety, where people don't automatically assume the worst about you."

He touched her shoulder in an uncharacteristically soft caress. "Would it help if I said sorry?"

Startled at the idea of him apologizing, she told the absolute truth. "I'm not sure."

"First, I get that call as I'm about to take off for Auckland, then I walk in and see you dressed as if you're waiting for a lover." His hand stroked down her spine to rest on the curve of her hip. "I may have jumped to conclusions."

"*May?*" she asked, struck by something else he'd said. "You were coming up here before Kayla called? I thought you were too busy."

"I made time."

A stubborn tendril of hope pushed its way through the hurt. Then Richard was suddenly beside her, wanting her to come say goodbye to several patrons. As a result, the next time she and Gabriel had any real privacy was when they stepped through the doors of the hotel elevator and began walking toward her room.

Her eyes resting on his face, she said, "I can't think what Kayla must be—" She came to a complete halt at her husband's muttered curse. "What's the matter?" She followed his gaze.

Her stomach curdled. Anything good that might have come about as a result of Gabe's unexpected apology had just gone out the window. Striding down the plush carpet, she faced the man slumped outside her door. "What are you doing here?"

Damon stood. "I wanted to talk to you face to face."

"I said what I had to say on the phone." Sickeningly aware of another couple walking out of the elevator, she tried to keep her voice low. It was hard—frustration and anger were exploding bullets inside of her. "I told you to go home to your wife." She slid her keycard into the lock and stepped inside.

Gabe hadn't said a word to that point, but he now put his arm on the opposing doorjamb, turning his body into a very effective barricade. "I think Jess has made herself very clear."

She placed a hand on his back. "Go, Damon.

Whatever we had, it's not there anymore. I don't know that it was ever strong enough to last." The time for gentleness had passed.

Rebellion spread across Damon's handsome face. "You're seriously choosing him over me? Jesus, Jess! Everyone knows you married him for his money."

"You know nothing about my marriage," she snapped, then tempered her voice at the open hurt on Damon's face. "Don't destroy our friendship like this. Please leave."

"So he can do to you what his father used to do to his mother?" Damon's shouted question attracted the attention of a maid coming along the corridor. The petite woman hurriedly wheeled her cart in the opposite direction.

"What?" Jess frowned, aware that Gabe had gone preternaturally silent. The hairs on the back of her neck prickled in warning.

"My mother used to work at Angel before the fire. She knows all their dirty little secrets!" He reached out as if to grab her from under Gabriel's arm. "I'm not leaving you here with a bastard who's going to put bruises on you!"

Gabe's fist slammed into Damon's jaw. The blow sent him to the floor. Crying out, Jess put herself in front of Gabe, her hands on his chest. "Don't, Gabe."

Hostility blazed in the green of his eyes and the dark red flush over his cheekbones. There was no question in her mind that Damon was sorely overmatched. In all honesty, she wasn't so sure she could handle Gabe either. But she was his wife. *"Please."*

He finally brought his hands to rest on the flare of her waist. Relief whispered through her.

Damon picked that moment to yell, "I'm not leaving till you tell me you don't love me!"

Jess felt everything in her stop. Her eyes met Gabe's. His hands dropped away and she swiveled to face Damon with a sense of destiny having caught up with her. The younger man struggled to his feet, rubbing his jaw and looking at her in a way she would have given everything for once. But that was then.

She blinked back tears. "I don't love you."

"You're lying."

"No, Damon." Shaking her head, she tried to make him see the truth in her eyes. "I'm not. I don't know if I ever loved you." She'd clung to him after losing her mother, her father and then her home itself. He'd been the last remaining part of her childhood.

His shoulders were so tight it had to hurt, but the anger seemed to be giving way to grudging acceptance. "You might not love me, but you sure as hell don't love him either. Do you?"

Her spine went stiff. "That's between me and Gabe. You don't have the right to ask me those questions."

"Jess?" Sheer disbelief.

"Go home, Damon. For God's sake, go home before you lose Kayla, too." As he'd just lost her friendship. How could she continue to respect a man who'd ignored everything she'd tried to tell him.

As realization dawned across his face she wanted to look away. He didn't give her the chance, striding past her in silence.

Sad for what had become of the wild but never cruel boy she'd known, she turned and walked into the room. It felt as if she'd severed the last safety rope tying her to the past. The future stretched out ahead. And it held only one certainty.

She was in love with Gabriel Dumont.

It had taken her far too long to recognize the feeling, blinded as she'd been by girlish daydreams of what love *should* be. She'd seen in Damon what she'd wanted to see, putting him on a romantic pedestal and spinning perfection out of fantasy.

Gabriel wasn't perfect, far from it. He could be so harshly distant and to expect tenderness from him would be to set herself up for disappointment. But still she'd fallen for him. Because while he might not be perfect, he was a man who'd stand by her through the tides, a man who'd respect his vows and his promises.

He was also a man, no matter what he said, who had the potential to both feel, and give, the deepest, most rare kind of love. The kind that came from the soul and left devastation behind when it was stolen away. She'd found her evidence in an acorn, a bunch of wild daisies and a smooth river-stone.

She wasn't so naive as to think he loved her, but Gabe *could* love, and love as women dreamed of being loved. If only he'd unlock that potential…but no, her husband was determined to dam up his emotions behind a barricade so thick, she was starting to lose hope of ever penetrating it.

The door closed with a click.

Giving a small start, she moved to stand in front of the uncurtained window. "I'm sorry about that." Gabriel was a proud man, one who wouldn't have appreciated passersby being privy to his private business.

"I think you broke his heart."

She couldn't tell if he was being sarcastic. "He'll recover. He always does." In many ways, her childhood friend was still that—a child. It was why she'd found it so difficult to break from him. Because so long as

Damon was in her life, she could pretend that nothing had changed, when the truth was...everything had. "And if he has any sense, he'll try to make his marriage work."

"Hard words." His hands closed over her shoulders.

"What do you want, Gabe?" Placing her palms against the glass, she stared out at the glittering city lights. "I admitted I don't love him. Isn't that enough?"

He massaged away her tension with fingers grown strong from a lifetime of physical work. "I'd never touch you in violence."

Jolted by the unexpected reference to Damon's accusation, she tried to meet his reflected gaze, but he was hidden in shadow. "What did he mean about your parents?"

"My father loved my mother," he said, his tone holding nothing of happiness. "Loved her so much he wanted her to be completely his. Even if he had to lock her in the basement to achieve that."

She put a hand over his, wanting to cry. Because she knew he never would. "Did he hurt you and your brothers and sister as well?"

"Angelica was too young," was his oblique answer. "He should've never tried to lay a finger on her."

"You were all too young."

"I don't talk about the past. It's dead and buried."

"But it has a way of rising up as we saw today," she said quietly, conscious that she couldn't force him to speak. "I'm your wife. Treat me like that matters."

Releasing her shoulders, he wrapped his arms around her waist and pulled her against him. When she closed her hands over his, she brushed the raw skin of his knuckles. "I never thought you'd be the type to punch another man." It seemed so emotional an act when control was everything to him.

"Violence runs in the family."

"You're too smart to accept such a facile explanation." She leaned fully into him, no longer fighting the effect he'd always had on her. Her body accepted him, knew him, needed him—sensuality was simply one aspect of that craving. "Anyone would have lashed out after what he said."

"Defending me, Jess?"

"I'm only telling the truth."

"So was Damon," he said after a long silence. "Though I suppose you could argue my father rarely ever actually beat my mother. He preferred to break her spirit in ways that didn't leave a mark. I think he'd nearly succeeded until that day when he tried to drag Angelica into the basement."

She was so worried about disrupting the moment she barely dared to breathe.

"My mother snapped, though I didn't know it then. That night, after my father passed out drunk on the couch, she gave us all a glass of milk."

"You hate milk," she said without thinking.

He hugged her tighter. "I didn't realize you knew."

"I told you, I'm your wife." And she'd keep fighting for that to mean what it should.

"My mother knew, too, and she didn't usually force any on me." His voice was calm but she read the emotional truth in the merciless discipline with which he held his body. "That day, I threw it into a planter when she wasn't looking.

"Then, after everyone else had fallen asleep, I snuck out to go exploring at a pond about a mile from the house. By the time I came back, the house was in flames and when I tried to run inside, the people who'd come to help dragged me out."

She ran a hand gently up his arm. "But you were burned."

"I was faster than they expected. Got into the hallway seconds before a beam collapsed."

"The fire," she whispered, a sick feeling in the pit of her stomach. "It was your mother."

Sixteen

"**I**'m pretty certain the milk was drugged. It was verified that none of the others had even tried to get out. And there was incontrovertible proof of the fire having been deliberately set." His voice didn't shake, didn't fracture under a load which would have crippled many men. "They assumed it was my father but I knew it couldn't have been. Once he passed out, he stayed that way for eight hours or more."

All she wanted to do was hold him. But would he accept the tenderness? "It was ruled an accident."

"It's a small town and the men in power at the time were good friends of my father's. They decided the truth would serve no purpose other than to make my life hell, so they buried it. It wasn't until I was sixteen that I pushed them to confirm what I already knew."

Stunned at what she'd learned and what it told her

about the man who was her husband, she tried to find the right words. "You're nothing like him."

"Enough, Jess." He brushed back her hair and kissed the soft skin of her nape. "I don't want to talk about this ever again."

It wasn't in her nature to give up, but they'd come so far today. Turning in his arms, she let him sweep her under in a dark wave of masculine heat. And for the first time, she didn't fight the surrender. In any way.

The next week passed by in a blur of happiness. Gabriel was no Prince Charming, but the man did have a way of melting a woman's insides when he decided to smile. And he'd been smiling a lot more often of late.

So when Jess ran into Corey at the grocery store, she felt terrible at being so happy that she'd forgotten the hardship he had to be going through…forgotten this aspect of Gabe's personality. Ruthless practicality might be part of her husband's nature, but it hurt her to think of him as callously unforgiving.

About to take the coward's way out and leave, she was caught off-guard by Corey's shouted greeting. Walking over, she smiled at both him and the little girl in his arms. "Hello."

"This here's Christy. My daughter," he explained, as if afraid she wouldn't remember.

"Nice to meet you, Christy. Your daddy's told me all about you."

The shy child half hid her face in her father's neck but Jess could see her smile. She felt even worse. "Corey, I'm so sorry about what happened."

Corey shook his head. "It was my fault. Mr. Dumont

was right to be piss—I mean angry," he substituted, glancing down at his daughter. "I would have been mad as anything, too, if that had been my wife and all. I wanted to tell you I quit. Smoking, I mean. For good."

"That's great." She was stunned by his lack of bitterness. "Do you still want me to do the sketch?"

"Would you?" At her nod, he grinned. "Could you do it from a photo?"

"Sure. If that's what you want."

"It's just that we won't be in town for long. I came back to pick up my mom and Christy. Needed time to set up things." His smile was very young. "The work's a little different with the vines and everything, but I think I like it even better than station stuff."

Relief rushed through her as she realized he must've found employment in a wine-making region. "Oh, I'm so glad for you."

"Anyway, we'd better be getting on home. It was nice talking to you Mrs. Dumont."

"You too, Corey. Good luck with your new job." She was about to move on when he slapped his forehead and stopped.

"I'm such a dolt." He made a face. "I wanted to thank you."

"Thank me? For what?"

"For talking to Mr. Dumont. I figured it must've been you." His expression was so sincere she felt her world rock on its axis. "If he hadn't called his friend in Marlborough, I might've been looking for work forever."

Jess somehow managed to nod. "Have a safe trip."

"Thanks. And don't worry, I won't stuff up this chance."

Watching him leave, she put her hand on one of the shelves and tried to steady her mind. Gabe had not only listened to what she'd had to say, he'd acted on it. Then why hadn't the dratted man told her?

Because he wanted to keep her at a distance.

So long as she thought of him as unnecessarily harsh, she'd never fully trust him, which played right into his hands. For her husband, a man who'd loved and lost everyone who mattered, her mistrust was far easier to accept than either her love or her care.

Jess's face cracked into a slow smile. Too damn bad for Gabe that she'd just found him out.

Buoyant after what she'd learned, she was almost ready to tell Gabe everything about her own feelings, willing to take a chance on the man she knew him to be. Perhaps she'd whisper it to him in bed, she thought, knowing she had to choose her moment.

"So," she asked after dinner that day, curled up on the sofa in his study, "do you want to know if it's a boy or a girl when I'm far enough along for them to tell, or do you want it to be a surprise?"

"I don't want to know."

"Really? I don't know if I'm going to be able to stand the suspense."

"That's not what I meant." He put down the fax he'd been examining. "I told you, I don't want to be a father. Don't involve me in anything where my participation isn't strictly necessary."

Staring at the implacable mask of his face, she tried to find some hint of softness. Of hope. "But Gabe, now that we've talked… You're nothing like him. You don't have to worry about hurting your child."

He circled his desk to face her. "Don't try and psychoanalyze me on the basis of something you know less than nothing about. I've made my decision."

Feeling dread chill her blood, she unfolded her legs and stood. "You can't mean that."

He ran a hand through his hair. "I won't ignore the kid if that's what you're worried about. I just want him or her around as little as possible."

"And how will being shipped off to boarding school and summer camps from such a young age make our child feel loved?"

His cheekbones stood out against skin stretched taut. "I'll take care of everything the baby needs."

"I see." And she did, far too clearly. "Love isn't part of the bargain?"

"It never was."

She flinched at the brutal execution of all her silent hopes and dreams. "I made that bargain for me. You're not going to cheat our child out of it!"

"I never lied to you about who I was."

"I thought—" She shook her head, furious at herself for having once again fallen for a man who'd only ever existed in her imagination. And this time, she'd gone far beyond girlish infatuation.

Horror drenched her at the thought of how close she'd come to declaring her love to someone who didn't want it and would throw it back in her face if she gave it to him. Wrapping her arms around her body, she told herself not to break down, not here, not now. "But men like you don't change, do they?"

"Why would you expect me to?"

Gabe's question from the night before echoed in Jess's mind as she sat on the steps to what had once been her home. However Randall Station no longer occupied that place in her heart. She'd accepted Angel in a way not even Gabe realized.

But it wasn't enough.

Touching the wood of the beloved home she'd thought she'd sacrifice anything to save, she shook her head. "Not my baby." Her child would not be held hostage to this place as she'd been, would not be forced to grow up alone and isolated in order to keep the Randall heritage safe.

And who had she been keeping it safe for but the life in her womb? Yes, it would break her heart to walk away, leaving her parents' legacy to the mercy of the developers. But that she could survive. What she'd never survive, what she'd never forgive herself for, was if she stood by and allowed her child to be torn from her arms in order to fulfill Gabe's inexplicable change of heart on being a father.

"I'm sorry, Daddy." She put a hand over her abdomen. "I'm sorry for not keeping my promise but I know you'll understand." A breeze whispered through the air to trail across her face, flicking away the single tear that had escaped her determination to be strong.

She'd been such a fool, first in thinking that she could survive a marriage based on nothing but business, and second, in seeing Gabriel Dumont as her very own knight in shining armor. He was no knight, not a man who'd ever be willing to give her what she most needed.

Perhaps the ability to love had been cut out of him long before the fire, his heart permanently damaged by witnessing his father's brutalization of his mother. Perhaps he'd lost it that night when Angel became an inferno that swallowed everything he'd ever loved. Or perhaps it was her he couldn't love. She didn't know the answer, but she did know that her child wasn't going to suffer for her stupidity.

Rising she walked down to the SUV and started it up. As she drove away, she allowed herself only a single backward look in the rearview mirror. Tears threatened to burst the banks of her control, but she resisted pulling over until she was out of sight of the house. Then she stopped. And let the tears come.

She was calm again by the time she reached the place that had become her new home. If there was one thing she didn't want, it was for Gabriel to see her as weak or pitiful. She was no longer that broken girl who'd begged him to save her home. Finally, she'd grown up.

Still, she was glad he hadn't yet come in when she entered the house. Going up to her bedroom, she packed a suitcase and carried it to the bottom of the stairs before heading to her studio. There, she began putting the bare essentials into a small bag. She'd get Mrs. C. to ship her her paintings after she found somewhere permanent to stay.

"What the hell are you doing, Jess?"

Closing the bag, she looked up at the man who'd become the center of her life in a few short months. "I'm leaving you." The pronouncement sounded shockingly blunt, but she knew no other way to make it without betraying the depth of her pain.

Green eyes glittered beneath the shadow thrown by the brim of his hat. "If you think this stunt will make me chase after you, you don't know me."

She drew in a ragged breath. "I don't expect that. We had a deal. I'm reneging with full awareness of the consequences." Tucking her hair behind her ears, she folded her arms and met his gaze without flinching. "I know you'll sell Randall Station. I'm not going to ask you to stop. It's legally yours."

"Your first payment under the pre-nup doesn't come due until we've been married two years."

She should have expected the cold-blooded response but there remained a foolish emotional softness in her, something that insisted on seeing the invisible scars on his heart, and that bled at his lack of feeling for her and their child. "I don't want your money." It inadvertently came out like the most severe kind of rejection.

"It'll take me a while but now that I have a source of income, I'll pay you back for L.A. Don't worry about maintenance for the baby, either. It hardly seems fair when you'd rather I wasn't pregnant."

"Don't be absurd, Jess." White lines bracketed his mouth. "I'm not having it said I threw my pregnant wife out on the street."

She picked up the bag with her art supplies. "Fine. Support the child, that's your right, but I don't want anything else from you."

He blocked the doorway. "Why the sudden about-face? You were perfectly happy with this arrangement a year ago."

She could have lied, but that no longer seemed an option. Maybe she'd had enough of hiding things, or maybe she was hoping for a last minute reprieve from a man who knew no such thing as mercy. Whatever it was, she told him the absolute truth. "A year ago, I didn't love you."

Seventeen

There was no reprieve.

Gabriel went silent after her confession and it took everything she had not to give voice to the anguish inside of her. Instead, she let him put her suitcase into the trunk of the SUV and when he asked where she was going, said, "I'll call you when I get there."

In truth, she had no idea of her destination. All she knew was that she had to leave. Driving aimlessly toward Kowhai, she thought about going to Merri Tanner, but disregarded the idea a second later. Merri was her good friend, but Mr. Tanner was Gabe's. It wasn't fair to put them in the middle of her and Gabe's problems.

In the end, she simply kept driving until night fell and tiredness forced her to check into a motel. Sleep was a long time coming. It was during those dark, lonely hours that she finally accepted the inescapable fact—she could no longer live in or around the Mackenzie Country.

Because in spite of its wide open sky, it was too small a community. She'd be unable to avoid hearing news about Gabe, unable to avoid running into him at area events. And she needed to forget him, needed to find a way to live without her heart.

Getting up early the next day, she drove straight to Christchurch Airport. After parking the car in the airport lot, she called Angel Station and left a message on the machine telling Gabe where it was.

Her second call was to another man.

Gabriel hung up the phone, trying not to crush the receiver in his hand. Jess hadn't called him. If the man she'd run to hadn't felt compelled to let him know that his wife was safe, he wouldn't even have known where she'd gone after she left the car at the airport *three days ago*.

Picking up the address he'd been given, he shoved it under a paperweight and tried to concentrate on checking some invoices. Jess had left him and she'd done it with a clear head. There was nothing to discuss—they'd had a deal and she'd broken it, though he knew he was to blame for that. He should have never tried to get her pregnant. Of course he'd support her as well as the child. He wasn't a man who ran from his responsibilities.

The pen snapped under the force of his grip, splashing ink across the invoices and staining his fingers a deep blue. Swearing, he threw the broken pieces into the trash and went to wash his hands. Afterward, he found himself walking not toward his study, but toward Jess's studio. He hadn't gone near that room since the day she'd walked out, but now he flicked on the light and began looking at the paintings she'd left behind.

Pride rushed through him at the depth of her talent. Her rural and city scenes were stunning but it was in portraiture that her skill became truly apparent. Life stories told in brush strokes on canvas, each paid painstaking homage to her subject—from a youthful Corey who was a cheerful sketch, to a laughing Mrs. C. in the kitchen.

The one of Damon was stacked with the others, a silent reiteration of what she'd said that night at the hotel. Jess had grown up, leaving behind both her innocence and her childish love for a man who'd never been good enough for her. And now she'd left her husband, too.

A year ago, I didn't love you.

Letting the portrait drop back to rest against the wall, he left the studio. But he couldn't escape the soft whispers of a feminine voice that insisted on speaking to him.

The sound of a car pulling up outside was a welcome distraction despite the late hour. Part of him was convinced that Jess had apprehended her mistake and returned. Hauling open the front door with enthusiasm he wasn't willing to admit even to himself, he walked across the verandah. But the woman who exited the gleaming sedan wasn't the one he wanted to see.

"What are you doing here, Sylvie?"

She waited for him to reach the car. "I got back tonight from a trip to Wellington. I heard what happened with you and Jess."

The sound of his wife's name made his entire body react with an explosive mix of need, denial and anger. She was his. She wasn't supposed to leave him.

"Gabe." Sylvie put a hand on his arm. "What we had was good."

"We were over a long time ago. I don't recall either of us crying tears over the split."

"We could have it again." Her voice was even but determined. "I'm ready to settle down and so are you. She just wasn't the right woman."

At that moment, Gabriel knew without a doubt that Sylvie would accept his decree to remain childless. She'd never ask anything more from him than he was prepared to give. That was how their relationship had always worked—two practical adults with little emotional investment in each other or their relationship. "No, Sylvie. You can't renew what was never there."

Her face blanched. "She'll never know you like I know you."

He'd had enough. "The single reason you know about the fire is because you overheard your father talking to the old coroner one night," he reminded her. "You never knew me." And nobody, not even her father, knew the real truth of who'd set the blaze.

Gabriel had told only one other person, the sole human being he trusted to never break her silence or use it against him. Because she was too gentle, too loyal, too damn loving. And he'd known that from the day he'd proposed.

"Do you really think Jess can ever be the kind of wife you want?"

The question silenced everything around him. "Maybe not," he said quietly, "but she's the kind of wife I need."

Sylvie's arm dropped away. "She's not here though."

No, she wasn't. He'd let her walk away. It might rank as the most idiotic thing he'd ever done but some mistakes could be rectified. Jess was his wife and she was going to stay that way. He refused to let her have her way on this one crucial point.

* * *

Jess had taken Richard at his word and not worried about finding an apartment for the week that he was in Australia. He had insisted she housesit for him when she'd phoned to ask about cheap rental accommodation. Leaving the night she'd arrived, he'd told her to rest and reconsider going back to her "beautiful shark." She'd thrown herself into work instead, doing sketch after sketch on a small pad she'd bought at a nearby bookstore.

And if her mind kept drifting to the last page in the pad, to the sketch she'd done first, at least she was able to stop herself from turning to it. Except at night. When her defenses crumbled and she gave in to the most awful kind of loneliness.

Conceding defeat after yet another long morning spent in a useless attempt to wipe Gabriel from her mind, she decided to walk the short distance to the gallery. Maybe Trixie, one of Richard's assistants, would like to go for a late lunch. It looked like rain so she hoped Trixie knew someplace nearby.

Pushing through the glass door of the gallery, she stopped dead at the sight of the man waiting inside. "Gabe?" Her whole body came to vibrant, turbulent life.

"You weren't at the apartment."

She fiddled with her purse, crushing that initial burst of wild hope. "Did you need to travel up here for a meeting?"

He looked very businessmanlike in his dark pants and crisp shirt. Except that it was *that* green shirt, the one permanently stamped with memories of his furious passion and her complete surrender. The emotional impact was devastating. But, of course, that wouldn't have occurred to him when he'd put it on.

"Yes, a very important meeting." Moving forward, he reached past her to reopen the door. "Let's take a walk."

She probably should have told him where to put his orders, but she was still so shaken up at the sight of him that she walked out without saying a word. It took the crisp winter-turning-to-spring air to slap her back to sanity.

"What did you want to talk about?" Facing him on the sidewalk, she tried not to let his presence affect her, a hopeless endeavor. Gabriel had affected her from the first—anger, passion, hurt…love. "Did you want me to sign something to speed up the divorce?"

A flash of some dark emotion sparked in the green of his eyes. "Trixie told me there was a park nearby."

She fell into step beside him despite her better judgment.

"Were you ever going to call me?" he asked, as they reached the narrow path, which cut between two buildings and led to the park.

She told herself she was imagining the edge in his voice. "I wanted to get settled into an apartment first. I thought it'd be more convenient for you to know where to send my paintings and things." A flat-out lie. She'd just been unable to bring herself to talk to him. The wound was too fresh, the hurt too close to the surface.

He thrust his hands into the pockets of his pants, shirt pulling tight across broad shoulders. Even now she had to curl her own hands into fists to keep from giving in to the urge to stroke.

"And you didn't consider that I might've been worried about you?"

The path ended. Needing time to think, Jess looked out over the empty green space. The usual crowd had probably been put off by the inclement weather. Clouds hung thick and heavy in the sky, threatening to break at any moment. But that thought was a momentary diversion—Gabe was waiting for an answer.

"No." She turned toward him. "I know I lie low on your list of priorities, somewhere beneath overseeing the reconstruction of the stables and above balancing your checkbook. Actually, I'm not so sure about that last one."

The skin of his face stretched taut. "Then why do you love me?"

Eighteen

Everything shattered. "I don't know!" she cried. "You're arrogant, emotionally shut off and far too used to getting your own way. If I had any sense at all, I'd stop loving you this instant."

Moving so fast she barely saw him, he grabbed her by the upper arms. *"No."*

"You can't control this, Gabe." She put her hands against his chest and pushed, her breath coming in jagged bursts. "I wish you could. Then everything would be exactly as you want, and I'd be happy right now instead of feeling as if I've been cut into a thousand pieces!"

He wouldn't let her push him away. "If you love me, why are you in Auckland? You could've stayed on Angel. You can come back today and I won't say a word."

"You know why I'm here!" She fisted her hands against the power of his heartbeat. "Even if I could accept living with a man who sees me as nothing more than a convenience—"

He kissed her. A passionate, hard, almost angry kiss that caught her unaware and swept her under. Thunder boomed in the sky but it was nothing to the fury of the storm raging inside of her.

"I need you."

She couldn't believe what she thought she'd heard. "Gabe?"

"You're the most inconvenient wife I could imagine." He cupped her face with work-rough hands. "You argue with me constantly, don't do anything I tell you to do, make me chase after you like a teenager with his first crush and keep sneaking into my thoughts when you're supposed to fade into the background. What the hell's so damn convenient about that?"

Her heart was pounding so violently, she couldn't hear herself think. "I'm not sorry."

"Of course you're not. That would be too convenient." He touched his forehead to hers. "Come back to me, Jessie. I don't think I can stand returning alone to that empty house."

She wasn't going to let him off the hook that easily. Jessica Bailey Dumont was through with settling for less than everything. "Why? Why do you want me to come home?"

"You're my wife."

"Not enough."

He hugged her close, tucking her head under his chin. "Stubborn, stubborn woman. You know why."

She was weakening under the weight of emotion in his voice, able to hear the words he couldn't say. But she needed this and if their marriage was going to work, he had to find the tenderness to give her what she needed. She wasn't sure he'd ever go that far. And then he did.

"I love you."

Her world stopped and when it started again, nothing was the same. Pulling back from his hold, she touched trembling fingers to his jaw. "Why do you make it sound like it's a bad thing?"

He stepped away from her touch. "Why do you have to question everything, Jess? Just accept that I love you and come home with me."

A drop of rain hit her cheek. "And the baby, Gabe?"

He thrust his hands into his pockets. "I can't give you what you want there."

The raindrop was joined by another and another, a cool mist in front of her eyes. "Why not?" She stood her ground, somehow knowing that if she gave in today, he'd never again permit her this close.

"Because I don't like children and I don't want one around." He bit off the words with cold precision.

"Liar," she whispered, wiping the rain from her face.

He turned from her. For a second, she thought she'd lost him and if she hadn't already been carrying his child, she might have accepted his decree. But she did have a life inside of her, a life that needed her voice to fight for its happiness.

The he turned back.

"They die." The words were flat, his eyes full of such pain she could barely stand it. "I forgot how easily children die until I saw you holding Cecily. They're small and weak and breakable. And I can't be there to watch over them every second of every day."

Everything became clear. Gabriel wasn't afraid of hurting his child, he was afraid of loving that child far too much. "But if you can chance loving me, why not our baby? I could be as easily hurt," she said, though she knew it wasn't what he wanted to hear. "There are no guarantees."

He thrust a hand through his hair. "Do you know how hard it is for me to accept that I love you? I lost four pieces of my heart in that fire. *I don't have much left.*"

Her tears hid themselves in the cool water flowing from the heavens. She began to reach for him but he spun in the other direction, going to his knees in the grass.

Heart breaking, she ran to him.

"I was their hero," he said as she knelt down in front of him. "I was meant to save them."

"Gabe—"

"You're strong, Jess, so damn strong. I can trust that you'll take care of yourself. But a child?"

"It terrifies me, too, this fear that something will happen to our baby," she admitted. "But I don't have a choice." Taking his hand, she forced it to her stomach. "And neither do you. This child will call you daddy, will look up to you and yes, will consider you a hero, because that's the kind of man you are. It's nothing you can stop."

He gave a violent shake of his head, wrenching away his hand. "No."

Just as frustration and panic threatened to smother her, she saw light at the end of the tunnel. "Gabe," she put her hands on his shoulders, "do you really think you'll be able to send your child, your very young child, to a boarding school, trusting that precious life to strangers? Will that let you sleep any more easily at night than having your son or daughter down the hall?"

His face paled. "Christ."

"You will love our baby," she began, intending to say that it was something neither of them could change.

"No." His shoulders tensed. "You're right about sending our kid away. I sure as hell won't be considering that anymore. But that's as far as I can go. Loving this kid is going to be your responsibility."

Jess decided to go with her heart. "All right, Gabe. All right." For the first time, she had the startling realization that she knew her husband far better than he knew himself.

The man had the gift of loving, loving so deeply and well it had almost destroyed him when he'd lost those he loved the most. And yet he'd admitted to loving her. His courage humbled her. That same stubborn courage would give him the strength to take their child into his heart. She had no doubts that the second he saw his baby, he'd realize that not loving that child wasn't a choice he could make.

"Jess." Cupping her face in his hands once more, Gabe kissed the rain off her lips. "If you ever leave me again, I'm not going to act so reasonably."

She laughed. "You call this reasonable?" She spread her arms to catch the rain but it was a hidden ray of sunlight that caressed her face.

"Damn reasonable." Getting up, he pulled her to her feet. "Come on, you need to get dry. We can't risk you catching a cold." And though he didn't mention why it was so important for her to stay healthy, she saw his gaze flick to her stomach.

Curling her hand into his, she smiled. Poor Gabriel, so used to getting his way. Little did he know that his most inconvenient wife was about to make his life even more unpredictable.

* * *

Jess had been wrong. Gabe didn't fall in love with their child at first glance. He fell in love with Raphael Michael Dumont somewhere between her eighth month and labor. Smiling at the memory of the horrified look on his face as he'd held their baby in the hospital and realized he was done for, Jess cut the peanut butter sandwich in half before handing it to the little boy jumping up and down by her side. "Here you go, honey."

"And Dad's?"

Prepared for the question that accompanied his every food request, she gave him the second half. Gabe had become used to being fed at odd times of the day and with food only a three-year-old would consider a delicacy. "He's in the study."

"I know." He ran off in that direction.

Picking up the tray holding her and Gabe's afternoon coffee and Rafe's hot chocolate, she followed at a slower pace. When she entered the study, it was to find her son standing beside the sofa where Gabriel sat. Rafe was laughing at something his father had said, but there was no laughter in her husband's eyes. In its place was a deep vulnerability that tore her up. It was gone a second later but she knew it remained inside of him. It always would, and whether he acknowledged it or not, it made him a better man and a wonderful father.

Biting into the sandwich he'd been handed, he ruffled his son's auburn curls. Rafe jumped up to sit beside him. Gabe rarely verbalized his love for his son, but Rafe didn't need the words. He had the solid confidence of a boy who knew he was loved absolutely and unconditionally.

Jess put the tray on the coffee table and sat down on Gabe's other side. "Are we disturbing you?"

"Every damn day. Can't get any work done."

Grinning, she wrapped an arm around his waist as he placed one of his over her shoulders. "Good. You'd get too stiff and grouchy if we let you alone."

His arm tightened. And she heard what he was saying. Like her son, she knew she was loved, loved so much that she was Gabriel's greatest weakness. "I think it's time," she said, having waited till after Rafe finished his snack and ran off to find a toy.

"He's too young."

"When did you learn to ride?"

He was silent for several minutes. "I'll teach him myself."

She'd expected nothing less. "We should use Maisy. She's gentle."

"The Tanners have a pony they're thinking of selling. Quiet, good-natured."

"Sounds perfect." She leaned against his strength, safe in the knowledge that the sole thing she had to worry about with Gabe and their son, was over-protectiveness.

"What did Richard say about your newest pieces?"

She grinned at the memory of her last conversation with the gallery owner. "He thinks you're my best piece, wants to know if he can borrow you as his date occasionally."

"I'll pretend I didn't hear that." Gabe scowled. "What about the paintings?"

"He said that aside from having an impeccable eye for hot men," she couldn't help teasing, "I'm also an artistic genius."

Gabe pulled her into his lap. "That explains why you married me." He caught her laughter with his mouth.

And she melted. The years since their wedding had

only intensified the sensual heat between them. "How can you always do this to me?"

A hint of familiar arrogance lit his eyes—Gabe might have decided to allow his family into his heart, but he was hardly tame. "I'm your husband. It's my job." A slow smile spread across that gorgeously masculine face.

She traced the edges of his lips. "In that case, I think you deserve a raise."

"Dad!" Rafe ran back into the study holding a toy. "It's not working." Unsaid was that he expected his father to fix it. That's what heroes did.

And Gabriel Dumont had always had the heart of a hero.

* * * * *

Happily ever after is just the beginning...

Turn the page for a sneak preview of
A HEARTBEAT AWAY
by
Eleanor Jones

Harlequin Everlasting—Every great love
has a story to tell. ™
A brand-new series from Harlequin Books

S pecial? A prickle ran down my neck and my heart started to beat in my ears. Was today really special?

"Tuck in," he ordered.

I turned my attention to the feast that he had spread out on the ground. Thick, home-cooked-ham sand-wiches, sausage rolls fresh from the oven and a huge variety of mouthwatering scones and pastries. Hunger pangs took over, and I closed my eyes and bit into soft homemade bread.

When we were finally finished, I lay back against the bluebells with a groan, clutching my stomach.

Daniel laughed. "Your eyes are bigger than your stomach," he told me.

I leaned across to deliver a punch to his arm, but he rolled away, and when my fist met fresh air I collapsed in a fit of giggles before relaxing on my back and staring up into the flawless blue sky. We lay like that for quite a while, Daniel and I, side by side in companionable silence, until he stretched out his hand in an arc that encompassed the whole area.

"Don't you think that this is the most beautiful place in the entire world?"

His voice held a passion that echoed my own feelings, and I rose onto my elbow and picked a buttercup to hide the emotion that clogged my throat.

"Roll over onto your back," I urged, prodding him with my forefinger. He obliged with a broad grin, and I reached across to place the yellow flower beneath his chin.

"Now, let us see if you like butter."

When a yellow light shone on the tanned skin below his jaw, I laughed.

"There…you do."

For an instant our eyes met, and I had the strangest sense that I was drowning in those honey-brown depths. The scent of bluebells engulfed me. A roaring filled my ears, and then, unexpectedly, in one smooth movement Daniel rolled me onto my back and plucked a buttercup of his own.

"And do *you* like butter, Lucy McTavish?" he asked. When he placed the flower against my skin, time stood still.

His long lean body was suspended over mine, pinning me against the grass. Daniel…dear, comfortable, familiar Daniel was suddenly bringing out in me the strangest sensations.

"Do you, Lucy McTavish?" he asked again, his voice low and vibrant.

My eyes flickered toward his, the whisper of a sigh escaped my lips and although a strange lethargy had crept into my limbs, I somehow felt as if all my nerve endings were on fire. He felt it, too—I could see it in his warm brown eyes. And when he lowered his face to mine, it seemed to me the most natural thing in the world.

None of the kisses I had ever experienced could have even begun to prepare me for the feel of Daniel's lips on mine. My entire body floated on a tide of ecstasy that shut out everything but his soft, warm mouth, and I knew that this was what I had been waiting for the whole of my life.

"Oh, Lucy." He pulled away to look into my eyes. "Why haven't we done this before?"

Holding his gaze, I gently touched his cheek, then I curled my fingers through the short thick hair at the base of his skull, overwhelmed by the longing to drown again in the sensations that flooded our bodies. And when his long tanned fingers crept across my tingling skin, I knew I could deny him nothing.

* * * * *

Be sure to look for
A HEARTBEAT AWAY,
available February 27, 2007.
And look, too, for
THE DEPTH OF LOVE
by Margot Early,
the story of a couple who must
learn that love comes in many guises—
and in the end it's the only thing that counts.

From reader-favorite

MARGARET WAY

Cattle Rancher, Convenient Wife

On sale March 2007.

"Margaret Way delivers…
vividly written, dramatic stories."
—*Romantic Times BOOKreviews*

For more wonderful wedding stories,
watch for Patricia Thayer's new miniseries
starting in April 2007.

HRFEB07

Hearts racing
Blood pumping
Pulses accelerating

Falling in love can be a blur…especially at

180 mph!

So if you crave the thrill of the chase—on and off the track—you'll love

SPEED DATING
by Nancy Warren!

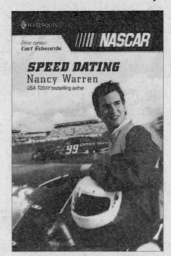

Hearts racing
Blood pumping
Pulses accelerating

**Falling in love can be
a blur…especially at
*180 mph!***

**So if you crave the thrill
of the chase—on and off
the track—you'll love**

SPEED DATING
by Nancy Warren!

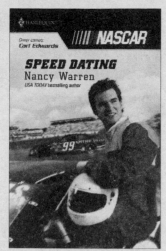

REQUEST YOUR FREE BOOKS!

2 FREE NOVELS PLUS 2 FREE GIFTS!

Passionate, Powerful, Provocative!

YES! Please send me 2 FREE Silhouette Desire® novels and my 2 FREE gifts. After receiving them, if I don't wish to receive any more books, I can return the shipping statement marked "cancel." If I don't cancel, I will receive 6 brand-new novels every month and be billed just $3.80 per book in the U.S., or $4.47 per book in Canada, plus 25¢ shipping and handling per book and applicable taxes, if any*. That's a savings of almost 15% off the cover price! I understand that accepting the 2 free books and gifts places me under no obligation to buy anything. I can always return a shipment and cancel at any time. Even if I never buy another book from Silhouette, the two free books and gifts are mine to keep forever.

225 SDN EEXJ   326 SDN EEXU

Name	(PLEASE PRINT)	
Address		Apt.
City	State/Prov.	Zip/Postal Code

Signature (if under 18, a parent or guardian must sign)

Mail to the **Silhouette Reader Service™:**
IN U.S.A.: P.O. Box 1867, Buffalo, NY 14240-1867
IN CANADA: P.O. Box 609, Fort Erie, Ontario L2A 5X3

Not valid to current Silhouette Desire subscribers.

Want to try two free books from another line?
Call 1-800-873-8635 or visit www.morefreebooks.com.

* Terms and prices subject to change without notice. NY residents add applicable sales tax. Canadian residents will be charged applicable provincial taxes and GST. This offer is limited to one order per household. All orders subject to approval. Credit or debit balances in a customer's account(s) may be offset by any other outstanding balance owed by or to the customer. Please allow 4 to 6 weeks for delivery.

Your Privacy: Silhouette is committed to protecting your privacy. Our Privacy Policy is available online at www.eHarlequin.com or upon request from the Reader Service. From time to time we make our lists of customers available to reputable firms who may have a product or service of interest to you. If you would prefer we not share your name and address, please check here. ☐

SDES07

This February...

Catch NASCAR Superstar **Carl Edwards** *in*

SPEED DATING!

Kendall assesses risk for a living—so she's the last person you'd expect to see on the arm of a race-car driver who thrives on the unpredictable. But when a bizarre turn of events—and NASCAR hotshot Dylan Hargreave—inspire her to trade in her ever-so-structured existence for "life in the fast lane" she starts to feel she might be on to something!

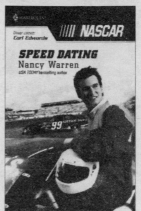